The Catacombs

Collected by Raven Black

The Catacombs

Collected by Raven Black

Hungry Goat Press

An imprint of Gauthier Publications

Cover Photo: Daniel Gauthier
Editing: Merideth Hadala
Book Design: Elizabeth Gauthier
This is a work of fiction. All characters in this book are
fictitious and any similarities are coincidence and unintentional.

1st Edition
Proudly printed and bound in the USA
Hungry Goat Press is an Imprint of Gauthier Publications
www.EATaBOOK.com

The Fountain

Careful the coin inside you place,
let not the statues see your face.
What is beautiful and safe by day,
turns to horror as the night gives way.
The statue was cast never meant for decor,
its meaning filled with terrible, forgotten lore.
The man behind its creation knew,
unearthly things, unfathomable but true.
Their cherub faces grow grotesque at night,
summon the monster that plagues this site.
So beware those among these cobblestone tread,
with a quickened pace you should have fled.
Drop nothing, leave nothing behind,
or come into your home, you they will find.
Run along now, go away.
In this place you are not safe to stay.

Raven Black

The Posioner
by Holly Day

$\mathcal{T}$he poisoner moved into the village soon after
the doctor had died. For weeks, she had been dropping
crushed narcissus bulbs into the doctor's drinking well
in the dead of night. Not so much that it'd kill him right
away, but enough that he wouldn't have to wait too long
to die. The doctor's wife followed soon after; her unborn
child spilling out on the stone pavers, brought out too
early by contractions caused by the poison.

    The poisoner came down into the village the very
next day, dressed in a white nurse's outfit; her clothes
paradoxically spotless considering that no one had
anything spotless to wear, not anymore. The war had
made everyone a dirty wreck, and the impossibly white
clothes of the poisoner made her seem a legitimate
miracle: some sort of savior coming down from the hills.
They would soon find that no matter how bloody she got,
her uniform would always be clean and white.

    If she had come down from her hiding place
dressed in her regular clothes, they would have cast her
out as one more hungry mouth to feed in a town with
nothing left to give. But dressed as she was, they gave
her the doctor's house, they gave her what little was
left in the doctor's pantry, they asked for her help. They
never asked where she came from, and when she said all

who had known her before were now dead, they took her past as a natural side effect of the war. If it hadn't been wartime, and she'd given the same answer, they would have questioned who had died, how they had died, why she had left. But since it was war, they simply shook their heads sadly and offered condolences.

Had they asked these questions, she probably wouldn't have told them about the babies buried in her garden back home; the babies that had died under her care in the hospital; the people she had poisoned much in the same way that she had poisoned the doctor. This was before the war, and she had been put in jail, and they were going to kill her. But then the bombs came and made a hole big enough in her cell for her to slip away and run. She had run and run, sleeping in old buildings and then in the countryside, run until she had found this town, with the phone lines out and the roads mined all to hell, and she knew she was safe.

And now she was the town doctor. She had an office, a bed, glass jars full of cotton balls and tongue depressors, needles, vials of precious morphine, antibiotics. If she hadn't come along, someone would have broken in here and killed themselves with the morphine. She hid the twenty glass vials of morphine under the now-her bed and pushed a pillow up against them, hiding them from anyone who didn't know what a pillow under the bed meant. She'd find a better hiding place later, when she was more settled in.

She was the new doctor, which meant that only healthy people came to see her. People with children, old people, sick people, they stayed at home and got sicker, older, more colicky, waiting to see what kind of doctor she was. You can't poison healthy people without incurring suspicion, so she had to be a real doctor for them. She set broken arms, broken legs, put tinctures on festering sores, stitched up wounds that could have just as easily been treated with plasters and antibiotics. Her patients went home happy, satisfied that she was indeed a doctor. Her skin itched from all the healing, but she was smart enough to know her place.

After a while, old people started coming by for aches and pains. New mothers would come in to ask why their babies kept crying. The poisoner counted, one, two, three patients; patients who could die simple, unnoticed deaths. Eight, nine, ten. Ten was a good, even number. She was a good doctor with ten vulnerable patients healed.

The eleventh patient was a man everyone called "Bobobri." Something to do with a vehicle he had once owned and the sound it made driving down the street— the poisoner wasn't sure about the story and didn't really care. She knew he was the one when he stepped into her office, that he was the one to stop the itching in her palms, the creepy-crawlies under her tight still-white nurse's uniform. Bobobri came into her office with an ache in his lower back and tremors in his hands, wanted something to stop the pain so he could keep working on his farm, or his car, or something—the poisoner didn't pay much attention to this information, either.

"I just want to make it through this damn war," Bobobri said as he sat down on the examination table, his breath wheezing as he raised his arms up over his head, turned his head this way, that way. "I just want things to go back to the way they were."

"Hmm," said the poisoner, nodding. She would shoot the morphine into his muscle right over his shoulder. He would be able to make the short walk home, sit down, maybe even fall asleep on his own before the morphine killed him. Or she could give him something to take orally right before bed: one pill with no written prescription. What would that pill be?

"I'm glad my wife never lived to see this bloody war," the man was saying as the poisoner searched the medicine cabinets for the perfect poison. "I'm glad my daughter went to America, so that she'd never have to see how I'm living now." He wiped at his eyes with the back of his hand and sniffled a bit. "We were so upset, especially my wife, that Ally didn't want to stay here. But now I'm so happy that she's gone."

"Ah," said the poisoner, pulling down a small vial from the cabinet and reading the label. Yes, this would work perfectly. She pulled a small plastic bag out of a drawer and shook three white pills into the bag. "It's hard work, being a parent," she said absent-

mindedly. She zipped the plastic baggy shut and handed
it to Bobobri. He took the bag from her and looked at it
curiously.

"No prescription?" he asked.

"Nope," she answered. "Three pills. Take them
tonight with water, right before bed, and come see me
in the morning." The poisoner smiled gently at Bobobri,
warmly, motherly. She would have hugged him if it had
been appropriate. She was already picturing what his face
would look like as the pills seized his muscles, stopped
his breath. His eyes would be frozen shut when friends
found him the next day, days later, maybe even weeks.
"He must have died in his sleep," they would say. "He
looks so peaceful."

"God must have sent you to us," said Bobobri as
he left the poisoner's office. He held the tiny bag with the
pills tightly, as if aware of the miracle contained within.
"We lost one doctor, and God sent us another."

"Call me in the morning," said the poisoner loudly
as she showed him out the door, so that anyone passing
by on the street would think she was truly expecting a
call. "Let me know if you need anything else, Bobobri,"
she added, and she meant it. She would do anything for
him, right now; her salvation from the itching of her skin
and the claustrophobic darkness pressing against her. He
was a pinprick in an oppressive bubble of solid darkness.
A pinprick that grew wider and brighter the further away
from her office he walked. The closer to his home he

drew. The waiting bed: his waiting death.

The poisoner spent the rest of the day consoling patients with minor injuries, cooing at babies, advising pregnant girls and single mothers widowed by the war. "Everything'll be okay," she said, over and over. She was surrounded by light now. She radiated holiness, healing, and everyone who left her office just knew things were going to get better for them, no matter what their circumstances.

It was nearly a week before she was called in to help remove Bobobri's body. The old man had fallen out of bed during his paroxysms, most likely right as the pills began to take effect, before paralysis set in. He was lying face-down on the floor by his bed, looking nothing like she had pictured his death would be. His eyes were frozen open instead of shut, a look of terror on his face. "Something must've scared him," said one neighbor. "Look how scared he looks."

"There's a lot to be scared of," the poisoner murmured, trying to decide if this sort of death was as satisfying as the peaceful death she had had pictured in her mind. Or perhaps it was more satisfying, because maybe he knew she had killed him, that maybe this thought was the last thought he held before slipping into death. He knew she had killed him, and he could do nothing about it.

Any time but now, someone might have called for an investigation into Bobobri's sudden death. His daughter might have come home, made demands, voiced suspicions. A neighbor might have heard his last, strangled sounds of dying, come in and checked on him, caught the poisoner's name in a last gasp. But no one heard anything over the constant rattle of bombs anymore, and he was old, so no one questioned her diagnosis. "Heart attack," the poisoner said. "Definitely a heart attack."

Days passed, weeks passed, and the itch came back. The poisoner checked in her log book to see how many people and children and babies she had not killed, and the number made her proud. Someone might think she was a real doctor from these numbers. The villagers trusted her because their children and their babies and their sick, elderly parents were not dying under her care. No one ever mentioned the pills she had given to Bobobri, or even asked about him. She had received a letter from his daughter in America, and according to the letter's instructions, the poisoner had helped distribute Bobobri's scant possessions to any villagers in need and mailed the few photographs left in his house to his daughter in America at her own expense. A family whose own home had been destroyed by bombing moved into Bobobri's house, and it was as though the old man had never been there.

But the itch was still there. It grew until the poisoner could feel the creepy-crawlies under her girdle, between her shoulder blades, in between her toes, all over the skin of her face. She spent her lunch break hiding in her bedroom, rubbing soap and hot water all over the itchy spots. She brushed her hair until her scalp was red, then tied her hair up so tight it stretched the corners of her face. And then she couldn't sleep, and she knew she had been good for long enough.

The patient was young, barely a woman, perhaps sixteen, and had been having trouble throughout her pregnancy, mostly hysteria-related. When her mother burst through the door of the poisoner's office screaming about blood and the baby, the poisoner knew it was some sort of sign: a harbinger of her relief. "Go back home," the poisoner told the mother. "Get some towels. Boil some water."

The poisoner pulled one of the precious bottles of morphine from under the bed and filled a syringe up to the top. Such a tiny, thin needle, so tiny the girl wouldn't even feel it going into her body. The poisoner stood before the mirror and slid the syringe into her sleeve. She looked at her reflection and could see the syringe. She slid the needle higher into her sleeve, practiced bending her arm, her wrist, with the needle concealed there. Pills were much easier, but she could do this. One pinprick in the base of the spine or the inside of a thigh and it would be done. One pinprick during the noisy, thrashing distraction of labor, and it would be done.

The poisoner slipped the needle into her pocket and grabbed her black medical bag. Besides a cursory show of interest in the baby's and mother's health with a dramatic flourish of a stethoscope, she didn't really need the bag for what she was going to do. But if she didn't show up with it, people would be suspicious. She knew how to play the witch-doctor role as well as any real doctor, knew the pantomimes necessary to allay a patient's fear.

When she got to the house, she was almost disappointed at how easy this was going to be. The towels the mother had spread out on the floor around her daughter buttocks were already dotted with blood, while the girl herself was obviously in real pain, beyond the pain of a normal birth. The poisoner ran to the girl to inspect her, putting on her practiced panic-face, shouting orders to the mother, "Get more towels! Where's the hot water? Put your hands here, here—I need more pressure here!" She shooed curious onlookers outside, finally sent the mother outside, called her back inside, waved her outside again.

"I could save you," the poisoner said out loud to the girl, the girl with the face twisted in pain, more animal than human in the face of agony. Yes, this was what she had missed, having her patients know she was going to kill them, or maybe save them. The slow light of recognition in the girl's eyes that the poisoner was talking to her, the realization of what the poisoner was saying. It's one thing to imagine your victim dying, alone in his bed, alone in his house. It's quite another to hold your victim's life in your hands.

"I could save you," the poisoner said again, louder. She pulled the needle out of her pocket and held it up to the light. She wouldn't have dared do this if the labor hadn't been so dramatic, so loud, loud enough to justify sending everyone out of the house, to send the mother hiding with her friends in the house across the street. She had freedom to put on a little show, the sort of freedom she might not have for years to come.

The girl saw the glass syringe glinting in the light and squealed. She opened her mouth and tried to scream, just as another contraction wracked her body. "Just... just..." she stammered before groaning and squeezing her eyes shut.

"The baby'll probably make it," soothed the poisoner. "If you die, but the baby lives, people will forgive me. The baby will probably live." She checked the progress of the baby. Almost there. If she gave the girl the shot now, the baby, still attached to its mother, might die as well. Her skin itched. Light filled her eyes. The blackness that always danced in her head roared beyond the edges of the light. The risk would be worth it. She plunged the needle into the vein in the girl's thigh and pushed the plunger down, hard. The girl's body shook; she managed one last high-pitched, awful scream, then fell silent. As her muscles contorted, then relaxed, the baby fell out of her body, alive. The poisoner quickly cut the cord, tied it up, and checked the infant's vitals to see if it had been freed from its mother in time.

"It's a boy," she announced, opening the door of the house to the crowd loitering in the street outside. Her neat, white uniform was covered in blood. She felt exultant, jubilant, frightened at the risk she had just taken. The baby fussed and croaked and whimpered in her arms. She held the wiggling, wet infant to its grandmother.

"I'm so sorry," she began. "I did everything I could for the girl."

The mother's eyes clouded over as understanding tried to force its way past her joy at holding the new baby. She shook her head slowly, choked back a sob.

"The baby's perfect, though," said the poisoner before the mother could say anything, could ask any questions, could push past her into the house to wail over the corpse of her daughter. "See how perfect he is? We should focus on this new, wonderful little life, right here; focus on how this new little life will need your love, your nurturing. We can't forget, in our sadness, how important this new little life is." The poisoner kept talking to the woman, numbing her, distracting her, until the woman finally looked up from her new grandson to nod and say, "I understand."

They buried the girl a few days later, no questions asked. The woman holding her grandson stood by the casket as it was lowered into the ground, fending off any condolences with, "I have to be here for my grandson now. This is all so awful, but I have to carry on for him."

The poisoner was filled with bright light once again. She smiled at everyone, everything. Birds seemed to be singing at her window every morning with the sunrise, the children playing in the street outside her office seemed only to have kind words and gentle laughter for one another. Her patients seemed truly appreciative of her ministering. It was a good place to be.

The war progressed almost unnoticed outside her window, a constant thrumming and shaking of mortar shells and truck bombs careening into the buildings on the outskirts of town. Occasionally, someone would be brought into her office that had been damaged by one of these bombs: a herdsman unlucky enough to be in the line of fire, a soldier found crawling through the streets, kneecaps shattered, half his face missing, or even bearing simple wounds that bled drastically. The townsfolk brought these people to her clinic, left them on her doorstep like sacrificial lambs, never expecting she could heal them but duty-bound to bring the sick and wounded to her door anyway. Her need consumed these lambs, satisfied her hunger, made her happy. She glowed when she walked. She knew all the children in town by name. She knew every ache and pain of every citizen over fifty. She brought more babies into the world, stitched up new mothers and sent them home.

The first prisoners were brought to the village after

the poisoner had been there almost a year. "We're just going to keep them here temporarily," the officer said. "Red Cross will stop by once a month to make sure they're being taken care of." A concrete bunker was hastily built by military personnel, none of whom had come from the town themselves. The poisoner stood with her people, watching the construction take place, wishing as she knew the rest of the townsfolk did that the military men would stay and help the residents rebuild the houses and storefronts that had been destroyed during the war. She watched as the first of the prisoners were moved into the small concrete bunker: a dozen or so weary, starving men who seemed more than happy to spend the rest of the war resting in a cell.

"We'll need a doctor to check them out," said the officer in charge as soon as the prisoners were contained. "There are reports to write up and file, reports on the captives' conditions to turn in to Red Cross." As he spoke, the poisoner felt a lightness growing in her heart. She finally knew she was exactly where she was supposed to be, that everything that had happened had been the will of some kind of God. She was in her place.
She raised her hand and waved it at the officer. "I'm a doctor," she said, smiling. "How can I help?"

The Barrel

by Holly Day

$\mathcal{F}$or as long as he could remember, the boy
thought the old wooden barrel was some sort of pet.
Three times a day, his father would take a jumbled plate
of scraps out to the back yard and leave it right at the
opening of the barrel. After the boy and his father were
finished eating, his father would go back out into the yard
and return with a plate to empty and clean. It was as
though it had been swabbed with a gigantic floppy tongue.

The boy often tried to imagine what it looked like
when the barrel was eating. He could see it from the
window of his bedroom, could just see what he thought
must be its black gaping hole of a mouth. Did a long, pink,
sticky tongue come out and delicately lap food off the
plate? Did some sort of hose protrude at mealtimes to
suck the food off the porcelain surface of the plate, like a
vacuum cleaner extension, or the way mouths of the tiny
tank snails worked in the fish tank at the doctor's office?
He could only imagine the answer, because whenever it
was time to feed the barrel, he was already seated quietly
at the table, waiting for his own food to be served.
He didn't dare ask his father if he could come out and
feed the barrel with him. He didn't dare ask his father
anything.

Sometimes, when the boy was outside playing,

he'd think about the barrel. The barrel was in the back yard, and the boy was only allowed in the front. A giant wooden fence surrounded the back yard. The only way into it or out of it was through the back door of the house. The boy's father was the only one with a key. "Stay out of the back yard," he'd say to the boy anytime he saw him looking at the big, locked door.

Once, the boy woke up in the middle of the night to noises in the back yard. He got out of bed and went to the window. His father was in the back yard, kneeling beside the barrel. He was saying something, but he was speaking so quietly that the boy couldn't understand the words. He thought he could hear noises coming back to the man from the barrel; noises that sounded like crying. After a while, his father stood up. He patted the barrel awkwardly before marching briskly back to the house.

The boy would often spend the long, empty hours of the day wondering about the barrel. He drew pictures and wrote stories on the backs of scratch paper about going to the back yard and making friends with the barrel. He was too little to go to school, and had no other children to play with, so his imaginary friendship with the barrel became his only friendship.

One day, his father caught him drawing pictures of himself and the barrel playing together. In the picture, the little boy was pushing the old wooden barrel on the rusty swing in the front yard. The boy's father's face grew red and angry as he looked at the picture. The little boy shrank into his chair, confused and frightened. His father was often angry, and the little boy had learned early on to stay out of his way. He did not understand why the picture made his father so angry.

"Stay away from that barrel!" his father finally shouted, crumpling up the picture and throwing it in the garbage. "Don't even think about the barrel!"

After that, the barrel was all the little boy could think about. He would lie awake in bed long after his father put him in his room for the night, waiting for the house to go quiet. As soon as he was sure his father had gone to sleep, the little boy would creep across the room to look out his tiny window at the old wooden barrel in the back yard. If he put his ear to the window, he was sure he could hear the barrel singing, or crying, or making wet, blubbery, nonsense noises to itself. Every once in a while, the barrel would suddenly jerk, just a little, as though trying to roll away.

During the day, the little boy tried his best to not think about the barrel. He tried to make up new imaginary friends to play with in the front yard; mostly other children like himself, sometimes fanciful talking animals. He'd give them all conspicuously manly names like 'Tom,' and 'Peter,' and 'Randall,' as his father seemed especially pleased with him when his imaginary friends had boy names. When he drew pictures of his imaginary friends, he made them all little boys like him, although, not having seen many other children, he often drew them with purple skin and green or pink hair. His father would frown slightly at these pictures, but since he didn't actually say anything, the boy went on drawing his imaginary friends in rainbow hues.

The night alone was dedicated to imagining about the barrel. In his dreams, the barrel sprouted legs and arms and could run about the yard like a person, or on all fours like a dog. When it was on all fours, it sprouted a long, wet tongue like a dog, and panted, and drooled, and barked. When it was on two legs, it laughed, and shouted, and said nice things to the boy, like, "You're my best friend," or "Do you want to run away with me?"

The dreams were so alluring to the boy that he began to think of ways to make them come true. The little window in his room had been nailed shut long before, but he began to see how easy it would be to take the nails out. He carefully dug at the soft pine windowsill in his room with the tines of a fork, and slowly, over the course of many nights, the nails began to come out. He was so careful not to make any noise. He was careful not to scratch the glass. He was careful not to scratch the wood too much with the fork, so that if his father happened to look at the window, he wouldn't see splinters and scratches on the frame. Unless he counted the nails left in the window sill, he would never know what the boy had been doing.

When all the nails were finally out, the little boy longed to push the window upwards. When he finally did,

the wood screeched so dreadfully his heart stopped.
He carefully, quietly, pulled the window shut again and
jumped into bed, waiting for the sound of his father's
footsteps. Sure enough, a few seconds later, the door to
his room opened and his father's silhouette filled the
doorway. "Was that you?" the man whispered. The boy
kept silent, eyes tightly closed, unmoving in his bed. After
a few seconds, the man turned away and shut the door
behind him.

As soon as he was gone, the little boy quietly crept
out of bed and went back to the window. This time, the
pane slid up easily, silently. The window gaped open to
the back yard. The barrel loomed in its corner of the yard,
its dark mouth open in a frozen scream.

The little boy squeezed out the window and tiptoed
across the yard. He could see his father sitting at the
kitchen table through the small window in the back door,
an open beer bottle in one hand, his attention focused on
the newspaper spread out on the table before him.
The boy held his breath and ran as fast as he could to
the barrel. Any minute, his father could turn around and
see him. He hoped he would reach the barrel before his
father turned around.

"Hello?" he whispered, dropping to his knees
and peering inside the dark of the barrel. It was much
larger up close than it had appeared from inside the
kitchen, almost as big around as he was tall. He could see
something moving inside, something way in back. He

crept closer, until his head was almost inside the barrel.

"Hello?"

Long, thin arms reached out and grabbed the boy. He squeaked and squirmed and tried to get away as the arms pulled him completely into the barrel. Pendulous breasts and long, matted hair brushed his skin. Thin arms pulled him close to a body that smelled horrible yet familiar.

"Shhh," whispered a voice near his ear. "Shhh, baby. Shhh."

"Let me go!" he managed to get out before a hand clapped over his mouth.

"Mine, mine, all mine," the voice began to softly sing. The body rocked back and forth, clutching the boy tightly, rocking him. "Mine, mine, all mine."

The little boy began to cry. He wanted out. He wanted back in his bed, the safety of his room. He wanted his father to come and get him, to rescue him from the stinky darkness of the barrel.

"Don't cry, little one," cooed the voice, still rocking, one hand still over his mouth. Finger combed through his hair, brushing it back from his forehead. "Don't cry. Someone will feed us soon."

Doom Dog
by Matthew C. Dampier

$\mathcal{T}$he first time I saw him it was well into the night and I told the on-duty nurse, "There's a dog in here." She didn't seem alarmed. It took her a minute to finish whatever she was doing and she weaved through the incubators to stand before me with hands on her hips.

"What can I do for you?" she asked.

"I said there's a dog in here. It sneaked through the door when the last couple left."

She made no effort to look around. She was younger than I was, which was an increasingly strange concept to wrap my head around as I neared thirty. Her skin, hair – everything about her – was pale white. Her hair pulled back was like a bundle of fiber-optic cable. You could tell she burned easily in the sun. From what I understood, nursing was the ideal vocation for those avoiding daylight.

"A dog," she said, incredulous. "When did you sleep last?"

"Me? Not since my wife woke me up to drive her here."

"Why not take a break? We'll put a cot in the room with your wife."

"I'm not tired," I lied. "She asked me not to leave the baby until she's well enough to come in here herself."

"That could be awhile. A Cesarean takes time to heal."

The dog came around the nurses' station and sat at my feet as if to beg. It was a small black dog – a mutt. One of his front legs was lame. His eyes were a sick yellow and when he blinked, fine strands of coagulated goop stretched between his lashes like melted cheese.

"Is this one of those healing pets you see on the news?" I reached down as a reflex to pet the animal, but reconsidered given the mangy condition of his coat. The nurse walked off without a word to hold a clandestine conversation on a phone with a tragically twisted cord.

The baby slept beneath her oxygen hood, eyes swollen and greased in ointment like an exhausted boxing champion. The heating lamp afforded her the rare pleasure of sleeping in only her diaper. She took her meals through a feeding tube crudely taped to her face which a tired, wrinkled hand now inspected with gentle suspicion. I watched the heart monitor, not knowing what I was looking for. The dog begged politely.

"How are we?" a doctor from nowhere asked. He had come in through an adjoining room where the well babies were kept.

"I was hoping you could tell me."

"Aspirated meconium is a tricky thing," his voice rasped. He had some throat condition he failed to mention – like he was always in need of a glass of water. It made everything he said that much more ominous.

"How much longer?"

"Until it works itself out. I'm concerned an infection

could present itself. We need to wait."

"So not today?"

"No, not today. Your wife was asking about you."

"How is she?"

"Perfectly fine. She's recovering from a routine procedure." The nurse was eavesdropping conspicuously from her station. "It's you I'm worried about."

"Me?"

"Are you aware that sleep deprivation is known to bring on hallucinations?" He glanced back at the nurse who was now pretending to file something away.

"Is that right?" I said. The dog was pawing at my shoes.

"A few hours rest would do you good," he suggested.

"I'll take that into consideration."

The neonatal intensive care unit housed those children born without the ability to cope with their new environment. The Earth did not want them here. The very air they breathed threatened to kill them, but with machines and needles and clear plastic tubes we made it possible for them, like spacemen, to live among us on this cold, angry planet.

There were couples worse off than my wife and I. They brought some twins in that afternoon. They could have fit in soup cans, and well should have for the way they mewed incessantly. The dog left me and navigated through the nervous, calculated mob of nurses to scrutinize our new roommates. He leapt onto a stool for a better view, yellow eyes wide like two soft-poached eggs.

While the nurses outfitted the squealing twins in their required uniform of IVs and coated copper wire, the traumatized father watched the scene through the blinds and chicken wire of the observation windows. Here bouquets, balloons, and eager friends and family became sick jokes. He was in a world entirely his own now, counting time down in tiny infant breaths.

Once the nurses were satisfied with their decorating job, they clicked on the heating lamps and left the now silent twins alone. The dog pulled back slowly like a spring and then leapt upon the foot of one of their beds, settling down into an uneasy roost, like a cobra eyeing a suspect rodent.

I stood up from the cheap, padded rocking chair and made eye-contact with the twins' father through the glass. "The dog," I mouthed. He looked confused. The nurse was in another corner of the room, folding receiving blankets. I walked over and tried to shoo the dog away. He bared his awful teeth and nipped at me. The father knocked on the window to get the nurse's attention.

"Can I help you?" she said, strutting over with an insulted look on her flushed face. The dog settled back into position, turning its head sideways, waiting for something.

"Sorry," I said.

"I'm going to have to ask you to leave for the night. The babies need their rest and so do you."

I knew that one call would bring up a pair of annoyed security agents and that likely I'd been banished from the maternity ward for good if I put up a fight.

"You could be right," I said, swallowing my pride like a razor blade.

Things were awkward in the hallway. The anxious father was fogging up the glass by his twins.

"What was that in there?" he asked without looking away from the babies.

"You saw it?" I asked, encouraged.

"Saw what?"

I lied carefully. "Spider was coming down its web."

"I can't see shit through these blinds. Thanks. I thought maybe you were losing your mind. You look tired."

"Just ready to go home," I said and joined him at the window. The dog's gaze was fixed on the smaller twin. Dad was young. He still had his hair and it hung like a hood over his ears and eyes. He was dressed in tight jeans and a band shirt. I was still in my ill-fitting scrubs.

"How long have you been here?" he asked me.

"Just one long day," I told him. "Fluid on the lungs. What did they tell you?"

"Severely premature and some other words I don't know."

"Where's mom?"

"Recovering from her C-section."

"Same here." He turned reluctantly from his babies and looked at me for the first time. "What do you do?"

"I'm a social worker. I hate it."

"I work at a bookstore. I hate it, too."

I feigned awe at the babies to get a closer look at the dog. "They're beautiful," I said, watching those insane, infected eyes that would never connect with mine.

"Boy and a girl," he said. "What have you got over there?"

"A little girl."

The girl was the smaller of the twins. She opened her eyes ever so slightly. This seemed to be what the dog was waiting for. His sharp black ears shot back like pistol hammers and the teeth came out again. He inhaled over and over again like a kid huffing a bag of glue. He was sniffing in a part of the child, undetectable by the human eye. It seemed to soothe him and when he had his fill he jumped back down onto the floor for a nap.

The baby's monitor blared out a sickening alarm. She writhed as much as her underdeveloped muscles would allow. The nurse came jogging over and the father raced to the window again. She reset the alarm. I startled her when we made eye-contact through the glass. I decided it was a good time to take a walk.

My wife slept. The pain medication had done her well. I kissed her forehead and left to ride the elevator down to the food court. Here it was difficult to determine if the food was bad because of your nerves, or because the food was bad altogether. I figured pizza was a safe bet and I sat, remembering how to eat, to swallow.

An older, heavyset black woman in pink scrubs was eyeing me from across the dining area. She picked up her pack of cigarettes and fountain drink to take a seat at my table.

"You the dog guy?" she asked.

I didn't answer her, only looked at her suspiciously.

"They said a tall, thin guy. Plus you've got the maternity ward bracelet on."

"I guess I'm the dog guy," I said, pushing away my tray, pizza untouched.

"Glad I'm not the only one that's seen that goddamn hell hound. They cut my hours and stuck me with the geriatrics after I called animal control on that dirty son-of-a-bitch." She took a big, long draw off her drink.

"Little black mutt?"

"Yucky Eyes, I call him. That's the one."

"What the hell is it?" She got wide-eyed and moved her straw up and down frantically. "Mmm – I don't talk about that kind of thing no more. I got a job to keep." She checked around for eavesdroppers. "I just wanted to let you know you ain't crazy," she whispered. She gathered her things and heaved up out of her chair.

"What can I do about it?"

"There's a man upstairs I can take you to see. Those damn dogs are all he talks about." She shook the pack of cigarettes at me. "First I gotta smoke."

The floor she worked on now was one above the maternity ward. Old men and women tiptoed around in loose gowns, dragging IV stands. We scurried past the front desk to avoid creating an excuse. She led me into a warm room where a man, maybe in his mid-fifties, sat on a bed covered by a stiff white sheet, watching television.

"Have you come to prod me again?" he asked the nurse.

"You're not that lucky. This young man's up from maternity. We gotta dog down there."

He motioned me in urgently. The nurse left and the door closed behind me.

"Sit down, sit down," he said, pointing out a chair next to the bed. He turned the TV off with a shaky hand. "New father?" he asked.

"Brand new."

"And the baby's had some trouble?"

"Her first breath was shit."

"Tough break. When did you last see the dog?" He put on a pair of greasy reading glasses.

"Maybe an hour ago. He sneaked into the NICU."

"Black, was he?"

"Yeah. A mutt."

"With sick, yellow eyes? Am I right?"

I nodded at him.

"They're all the same breed. Doom dogs. Places of death – places like this – draw them like flies.

"Why can't everyone see them?"

"I don't know for sure. Those of us who can must have something in common."

"What do you know about them?"

"Never look the bastards in the eye. That's the main thing. I've got a big one there behind you in the corner. He's been trying to catch my eye for years." I looked behind me at the empty corner. "Don't worry. He wouldn't waste his time with you. It's the old stuff the big ones want. Maybe death just thinks we're all big bottles of wine. Finish one off and pop the cork off another. This one's just about got me. My damn blood pressure. He's already gotten me twice."

"How do you mean?"

"Three looks. That's all they need to suck you down. The big one there, he comes around when my blood pressure is up. He wants to catch me off guard. They're patient like that. He'll just sit and wait for me to lose my composure."

"You can't get rid of them?"

"You can get well. They'll lose interest then and go off to find an easier cork to twist."

"One of the twins downstairs got an eyeful."

"You're lucky the little ones don't open their eyes much."

"So this mutt, he takes the twins and then he's on to my child?"

"Unless she gets well before then, or unless you can

glue her eyes shut." The patient looked at the door suddenly. "My big boy's run off now," he smiled. "I must be pulling through."

I peeked out the door. The nurses were all headed down the hallway toward another frantic alarm. My new friend came waddling by with a stethoscope around her neck.

"You got to go," she wheezed.

I shut the door.

"Finally," the patient said. "Someone older and sicker than me."

"You can get them off your scent – just like that?"

"Not for long."

"And will they leave this place?"

"I doubt they'd leave behind a guaranteed meal. I've never seen one out in the world."

"Good luck," I told him and checked the hallway again. The nurses were quiet now. The alarm was dead like the patient it was plugged in to.

"Remember," the man said. "Three looks. That's all you get."

The young father was asleep in a chair. I checked on the twins through the glass. They had skin like dried fruit and their chests fluttered sporadically. No sign of the doom dog. My daughter was sleeping peacefully. Her color had much improved. There was a new nurse on duty, a redhead. The way she glared at me from her station made me certain she had been warned about the man and his dog. I kept my distance. I found an empty chair in the waiting room and closed my eyes. Sleep took me eagerly.

It could have been five minutes or five hours. They only way to tell time in a hospital it by who's on duty – watches make no sense here. It was still the redhead. She was in the NICU with half a dozen white coats removing wires from the smaller twin. He was lifeless and gray. The father had waited his turn and now that the doctors were through they allowed him to hold the limp thing in his hands that was supposed to be his son.

The doom dog sat in a rocking chair, bloated, licking his paws. His efforts had paid off and it was evident that he had increased in size. Even his coat took on a healthier sheen. If only the father knew that one of Death's dogs sat a few feet away leisurely preening its claws, he would take him by the throat and squeeze the stolen life out of it. The young father wouldn't have noticed me, deep as he was in despair, but I decided that the rest of this moment was better left unseen. The doom dog slept, pus dripping from his closed eyes like thick mustard.

"They brought you a cot," my wife said from a fog.
"I'm not tired."
"How's my baby?"
"Better, I think. The doctors were busy. One of the

twins died."

She was asleep again. I had watched them open her up like a carry-on bag to dig out the baby.

The view from our recovery room was poor. All you could see was a section of the roof and a small triangle of the night sky. They didn't want you to fall in love with the place, even though the cost per night was more than the best resort in Mexico. Something was wrong with my left hand. It was stiff and purple on the places it came in contact with the dog. Touching him for that brief moment was like plunging my arm into a cooler to fish out a drink. Still it stung. A few of my nails were loose in the bed. I was able to wiggle them like ripe baby teeth. It was frostbite plain and simple. Would the scent of my now dying fingers bring the dog, I wondered. It was no mystery why he took his meals with his eyes. Any direct contact would spoil his intended meal. Perhaps now I was a rotten fish to be ignored. Fine by me. I would have to find him something more appetizing and bring it to him on a silver platter.

I quit watching the sunset in our little triangle of sky and collapsed on the musty cot.

A sliver of sunlight cut through the room like a hot scalpel. My wife wasn't in the bed. In the hallway an orderly pushed along the morning meal cart. I found my wife in the NICU. The nurse buzzed me in reluctantly. The baby slept in my wife's arms, wires trailing back where she was tethered to the monitor. The doom dog lay at her feet like a loyal pet expecting a well-deserved treat. He was larger again. I scanned the unit.

"Where's the other twin?"

"Passed this morning," my wife whispered, ashamed at the joy of holding her child for the first time.

"They've gone home," the nurse interrupted. I wasn't sure if she meant the parents or the twins. I jammed my black hand in a pocket.

"Aren't more babies being born?" I asked the nurse. "Seems empty in here."

"Slow week," she said, smiling, and went back to her work.

I kneeled by the dog surreptitiously and showed him the dead hand. He sniffed it curiously. I thought for a moment I could convince him I was nearer death but it was useless. He wouldn't look me in the eye. I wasn't a meal worth waiting for.

"You can't be coming up here whenever the hell you want," she said.

"I need to see him." She looked around for her co-workers who were all evidently occupied with some other task.

"Ok, I'll take you up. But go easy. His pressure's up again."

He was curled up in bed, staring at the floor. "Got a bad one in here," he muttered. "Biggest I've seen."

"Would you look at this?" I said, and showed him the hand.

"I told you there was no touching them."

"You didn't say it would turn my hand into a burnt match."

"I made the mistake of kicking a doom dog ten years ago." He lifted up his stiff hospital blanket revealing a stump. "Get me into the wheelchair," he said, repositioning himself in the bed. He kicked over a tray of pills and they scattered on the floor. I knelt down and picked them up one by one. It took some effort, but I got him into the chair. "Let's go," he said.

"Where to?" I asked him.

"I want to see that baby of yours."

"What about your dog? Won't he follow you down?"

"No. He'd only follow if he was worried about losing his meal. He knows I'll be back. Big dogs like him don't follow. They wait."

I told the woman at the front desk he was my uncle and she let us into the maternity ward. My wife was in the hallway tottering in an awkward, painful way.

"What are you doing?" I asked her.

"We're going home today," she said. "I came to tell you it's time to collect my things." Her face was red and cheerful. "Who's this?" She asked of the man I pushed in the wheelchair.

"I'm here to see the babies."

"It is like a zoo, isn't it?" she said with a quirky grin.

"You have no idea," he said.

"I'll meet you in the room," I told her.

A doctor stood inside the NICU filling out paperwork with the nurse.

"Those are discharge papers, I hope," I whispered.

"I can't see a damn thing from this chair." He strained his neck. "Where's the child?"

I went and stood at the window above her bed and glimpsed the dog growling with his white, hot eyes.

"Dammit, it's back!"

"Don't wake the baby, we might have her out in time. The doctor stood with a clipboard at his side, shooting the shit with the nurse. The baby opened her eyes slightly and the dog edged forward. "God dammit!" I yelled. "I'm going in there!"

The man reared back in his wheelchair, frantically twisting the cap from his blood pressure medication. I went and banged on the NICU's door with my charred fist. I saw them through the small rectangle door, whispering no doubt about the likelihood of my insanity. I banged again and the doctor picked up the phone to call security down to drag me away. I looked for something solid, anything that could break through the chicken wire and glass, but there was nothing but heavy plush couches and nailed down tables with magazines.

The only thing I could conceive of shattering the

window was the man's wheelchair. He sat in it shoveling pill after pill into his mouth, gnawing them disgustedly.

"What the hell are you up to?" I asked him, exasperatedly.

"I'm helping."

The baby was staring, perhaps now aware of the creature that sat at her feet, hungry for her last breath. But now the dog averted his eyes. He leapt over the baby and rested his paws on the glass. The man had captured his interest.

"What's happening?" I asked him. He didn't look good. The glass cracked violently and the dog soaked through the glass like snot through cheap tissue. He bounded onto the floor leaving only a greasy translucent smudge behind him. The old man squeezed his eyes shut.

"Back up," he said through gritted teeth. The dog sneered and drew in great breathes, tasting the weakness that pervaded his chemically stricken body. This was a bite he could chew. "Back up," the man said again. I wasn't sure if he was talking to me or the dog. It leapt into his lap singing what remained of his thighs. The man opened his eyes. The two of them locked into a hypnotic gaze. The dog was euphoric.

"Back up," the main said once more and this time he pointed a crooked finger in my direction. I took a few reluctant steps back. There was an exchange of what could have been liquid or light or both draining from the man's mouth and nose and pouring into the dogs eyes.

A stain was forming in the ceiling panel above this flickering murder scene. It started as a dark, baseball sized water stain and grew into a large yellow and brown warped mass as if a filthy tube had overflowed on the floor above us. The massive wet head, and then the front legs of a gnarled and marbled Great Dane descended from the spot and quickly the entire body was lowered onto the tile by a disintegrating web of mucus and decay. The Great Dane stretched and shook the slime from its great bristled coat and took the smaller dog within its jaws and swallowed it like an anaconda would a paralyzed rabbit. The light show ended for only an instant before this new conductor struck up the final scene.

What life remained in the man was taken in for dessert and then the Great Dane was carried up into the ceiling panel again by an organic pulley system of sinew and varicose veins. The telltale stain quickly faded away.

Security arrived as it always does at the worst possible moment. The man lie, head back and eyes wide and steaming almost imperceptibly.

"Sir, is there a reason you're banging down the NICU?"

"This man needs help," I said numbly. Now their attitude changed and the doctors came from hidden doors to confirm what I had already known.

"He's dead."

Nervous men in suits came soon after, perhaps to determine who was at fault for this embarrassing oversight.

"If it's all the same," I told them, "I'll take my daughter and go." The discharge process was streamlined with amazing speed.

The nurse pushed my wife and child down the final hallway toward the humid warmth of the outside world. The last pieces of my hand crackled and fell away like cigarette ash.

"What happened to that man?" My wife asked as we breached the automatic doors.

"Some people get sicker when they go to the hospital."

Mail Order Mud

by Karen DeCapp

"*Y*ou're a cripple."

He'd been called worse.

"You're a freak."

Still heard worse.

"You're stupid."

Now they were just wrong. Emotionally crippled. Terrorizing freaks. And oh, so stupid. But they'd learn. They'd learn.

With a club foot, lazy eye, and spastic bladder, Brian Holton, unwillingly, had been assigned hell. The bulk of the assignment administered between ages six and eighteen. He was now twelve. Midway through. And even at twelve, he comprehended the dangerous midway marker. Little Red Riding Hood midway through the forest met the Big Bad Wolf. Dorothy encountered the Wicked Witch of the West midway down the Yellow Brick Road. And Jack tripped midway up the hill fetching water. Coincidence that malaise, maniacal, massacre, menacing, and misery share the same segment of the dictionary with midway? Fables indicated no.

Recess existed for the welfare of young minds. Brian referred to them as quarry quarantine. Restricted ground, enclosing packs searching for prey. One prey.

The prey with the most abnormalities. Bad eye, limp walk, several trips to the bathroom. Don't need to look too far. Four eyes, brace face with freckles, Jenny Donner, was a distant second. Once she started to develop, japes turned to gapes. Brian didn't have that out.

He was a seemingly uncomplicated, non-creative little boy restricted by his physical misfortune. Much like dyslexia held back Thomas Edison.

As time went on, the quarry expanded. No longer did quips begin and end on the schools four square painted blacktop, chalked hopscotch, and basketball hoops without nets playground. Now the burliest bully, Doug Thorr, put in over-time. His high-top tennies, pierced ear, and shaved haircut nearing a razor swipe, pushed boy to man, and harassment to hazing. Except little by little his teammates were dropping off. Sports, grades, girls, collectivism beyond detention halls.

On this Wednesday in May, blue sky, one cumulus cloud in the shape of a snowman, swift breeze, steady traffic flow, Brian walked home on the sidewalk. Doug, confidently, slowed Brian's stride from the front, and Skip Nelson and Will Shane dogged him from the rear. Not even this blusterous May day shook a fluffy flake from the cumulus snowman. Odd.

"Should be home by...what...midnight?" Doug's arm's waved with his words, eyes glanced to Brian's right foot dragging the pavement, while his reversed stride stayed in rhythm and Skip and Will laughed right on cue. Laughing at Brian meant not being a butt of the joke. At least, not at this moment.

Twenty pounds overweight, Skip no longer skipped to the ice cream truck. He waddled. He also used a portion of his allowance to buy a cone for his skinny sister who ran and stopped the faded white van for him.

The word 'comply' tripped up Will. Though he lived it, on an exam he spelled it with a 'K' and flunked usage. He also had trouble using a straw, and fainted twice during gym. Probably because of nerves and dehydration. But with Brian around to pick on, no one noticed.

Brian kept his head down, but his bad eye wandered.

The boys were nearing the corner where Brian turned. His house sat one away. Picket fence, flower box, Herringbone brick pavers to the front door. Sweet, simple, refuge.

To prevent a possible confrontation with Brian's mom, Doug made one last remark. "You're a complete freak." Then ran by Brian, giving his shoulder a shove. Brian briefly stopped to gain his balance, turned and watched the three trot down the sidewalk in single order. Skip, a distant third.

Brian then noticed Andy Schaffer on his bike on the other corner to his left waiting for the light change and observing the teasing. Andy left the menacing montage months ago. Why Andy went rogue from the bunch was unsure. No sense analyzing a positive. Brian made the turn home and kept walking.

The traffic stopped at the intersection, a tinkling of a bike chain, and then Andy rolled his bike to Brian's side. "Hi."

"Hi." Brian lowered his head again. Twenty steps he'd be home.

Andy pedaled slowly to keep at Brian's pace, standing straight to achieve it. "Skip and Will might stop being mean, but Doug...well...he's an ass." Andy looked around as if his mom, two miles away through an open window, tuned up her supermom ears to catch his curse word. He waited for the scream to get home. It didn't happen.

Brian stopped, mainly in disbelief, partly to absorb a hint of friendliness. "What?"

Andy braked and straddled his bike. "Skip and Will. One of these days they'll see how mean they're being. Well, hopefully. Doug knows how mean he's being and loves it. Nothing will stop him. He'd be mean in jail. 'Cept then, someone will be meaner."

Pause.

Then Andy continued. "Sorry. In the past I've been so mean to ya. You don't deserve it. No one does."

Speechless, Brian nodded a thank you.

"My little brother, Tad, has started talking with a lisp. Kids mock him."

"Sorry."

Andy returned the nod.

"Doug's meanness goes deep. He goes out to Camp Phister...do you know Camp Phister? Boy Scouts used the cabin for retreats a few years ago."

Brian turned to his house. "It sits a half mile from my back door."

Andy gazed over as if looking through the building, past the ravine, into the woods, and seeing the small log cabin. "Yeah! Doug goes and tries to find birds nests to steal the eggs and smash them. Worse yet, he traps squirrels in a cage using snickers and takes them back to his garage. Don't know what he does with them, but the neighbors hear awful screeching. Police have even been called."

"How disgusting."

"Ever go to Camp?" Andy asked.

"Nah." Shuffling foot, blurred vision. Not a hikers dream. Club foot, one in a thousand. So was catching a fly ball at Yankee stadium. That didn't occur. Didn't happen at the minor league game either. One in a hundred. Odds only worked against Brian.

"Gotta go. See ya around." Andy pedaled off, standing and swaying the tires to and fro.

"Yeah, see ya." Brian called and waved to Andy's back, lost in the enthusiasm of banter and not barrage.

Entering the house, Brian's mom stood at the sink dunking objects in water and placing them in a wire container to dry. For three weeks the knick-knacks were feather dusted, the fourth week dipped and cleansed. Though this gave the illusion of finicky housekeeping, the ritual was limited to two Limoges vases with lids. All other items and shelves displayed 'we're not having company' complacency. Clearly, the expensive 19th century look didn't mesh with gritty Americana circa 1990. But next to Brian, the Limoges vases were her most prized treasure.

"Hi Sweetie." A brief look, wink, and she returned to the delicate porcelain. The lapse exposed her deep love for him. Hundreds of dollars in her slippery hands, and she visually greeting him. "Did you have a good day, dear?" An invitation to sit down and talk conveyed. Sometimes it worked, sometimes it didn't. As Brian got older 'the didn't' outnumbered the 'worked'.

"It was alright. I'm going to go to my room."

"I'll let you know when supper is about ready. Do your homework, sweetie."

He wasn't good at following directions. Without a response, he opened the door to his bedroom. The door always remained shut. Whether he was inside or out--- shut. No lock was installed, just the message of privacy. The request for respect. Honoring the message, instead of enforcing it, held the highest level of regard.

Brian flopped on the bed, put his hands behind his head, and stared at the poster on the wall. An average tree in an average forest with average shrubs, leaves, a stream of sunshine breaking the tree line like laser beams from ten rifles. Of course, that was to the average eye. But the poster came from a Mud Man comic book. Special collector's edition. $14.95 compared to $6.95.

To a simpleton, the sturdy Oak in the background with a brown textured base, multiple knots, housing a large hanging oriole nest embraced the peacefulness of the forest. In the lush mix of fluctuating green were the red and white of high bush cranberry, winterberry, and red-osier dogwood. Beauty and bounty. Growing wild, feeding its inhabitants, and asking for nothing but respect. I think I shall never see a poem as lovely as a tree.

To a trained eye, and connoisseur of Mud Man memorabilia, such as Brian, Mud Man disguises himself to protect defenseless nature. Stop the killing, halt the butchering, contain the fire, and mind the trash.

Mud Man had metamorphosed into the mud packed, twig laden nest hanging from the oak. At different moments he was the mud covering the roots, the soil enriching the hardwoods, and the clearing seen but not crossed by hikers. Batman drove a car, Superman flew, Spiderman climbed buildings, and all had alternate lives. Mud Man had one objective, one motive, and visitors to nature had only one directive. His motto, I think I shall never see an encroacher at a tree.

Brian didn't care if some considered Mud Man comic book violent, morbid, graphically poetic. Mud

Man only harmed those doing harm. He'd consume them into land, to be useful. The mutant evil human element, transformed into a resource of nature.

Questions rose within him, if the end justified the means. Certainly not to his Limoges-vases-cleaning mother. Brian hid the books in folders marked 'Sixth Grade Science'. Fearing courses of dissection, his mother didn't investigate. Academics or leisure, she abhorred animal experiments. Cringed spraying the house of ant repellent. They were living creatures. The sentiment, a shared gene. However, Brian found one species warranted dissection.

He retrieved the latest issue of 'Mud Man'. Eerily, Mud Man smiled clinging to a tree, one tree out of dozens, in the mysterious climate of high sunlight and low fog. Each particle reaching to overtake the other. A twisted version of Waldo.

In the hazy battle, only a smidgeon of teeth by the top gum line flashed ivory. Only the outside corners of the sclera peeked from the bark. Easily dismissed as fungus, insect infestation, or 'muddled' effects of vapor, intruders trample the grounds in his midst. Unaware. Unafraid.

"I see you," whispers Brian.

Then a knock at the door. Though slow on his feet, Brian's hand moved with a magician's quickness. The comic book sliding under the bed covers as if a white rabbit sprang from the cloth.

"Yes?"

"Honey, a box came for you. May I come in?"
Again, respect is granted for entrance.

"Yes, mom. Come on in."

She entered. In her hand, a box which might have
contained a medium pizza. It did not. Stored an array
CD's. It did not. Or a framed piece of artwork. Another
negative.

His body language delivered a powerful blast of
excitement. Popping from the bed, arms outstretched,
vision locked, he accepted the box, demanded the box, as
a mother longing for her first child. Nurse, pass me my
baby.

"What have you ordered, Brian?" The label read
'MMM-- Read directions carefully.'

"It's...it's for a school project. Extra credit. Very
intricate."

"Okay. But be careful. The label says to read the
instructions carefully. Be sure to mind the directions."

"Yes, mom. I'll be careful." He was never one to
follow directions.

As his mother left and the door latched, two of
the four taped sides of the box had been ripped from the
cardboard. The other two stuck as if glued, forcing time
and consideration to the content.

Gathering scissors from the desk drawer, he lightly
cut the tape holding the box closed. With the final strap
of concealment severed, a loud snap commanded the

room. If the lid of Aladdin's lamp had lifted, smoke and a jeweled turban would stand before Brian presenting three wishes. Alas, it did not. Nor did enchantment or a dancing girl. Instead, a weight loomed.

No tissue, foam, or plastic guarded the contents. None required. If a person ordered this item, they understood the power. Torpedoes and bombs don't have protective coating, fancy paint, stamped warnings. Neither did MMM. MUD MAN MATERIAL. Offered only once. In the Collector's Edition. In the back—far back, behind the malarkey monkey's tail, elephant ivory, and rabbit's foot. Items of scourge and pestilence to Mud Man. He'd no sooner encourage the demise of nature's habitants and ownership of animal parts and carcasses, than produce a parking lot in a field of lilies. Beauty is raw, ugliness is processed.

Six objects sat unadorned in the box. The ad as quaint and prolific as pumpkin seeds. But can everyone harvest a pumpkin? One must be diligent, watch for prickly leaves, and keep the bugs at bay.

In small, cursive print was the ad 'Special mud, reap the benefits; explore the wild---LIMITED TIME FOR A LIMITED FEW'.

Utterly criminal the approach. Even more diabolical, the price, $9.99. Purposely, less than the special edition, much less than a monstrous electronic toy, destroying the mind with sound waves able to pop corn and instill tintinnabulation. Brian preferred the quiet scepter of cognizance. Who would ever surmise the miracle of Mud Man came in a pizza box for $9.99? Only the people who searched the quiet and found a conventicler innately concealed within the urbane. One being Brian Dunston. Mud Man Devotee.

Without an exhalation, Brian gently, removed the objects as if nuclear detonation would occur with a sudden jerk or air density change.

First, the miniature hand rake. Wood handle, metal prongs, Lilliputian gardening scale. Second, a slightly mashed paper cup, the size of a cough syrup lid, lunch bag thin, and so delicate, so obvious it'd have limited use; eye and hand contact threatened its sturdiness. Third, a wire hoop, with a 14 inch circumference and twelve thick organic cords, resembling raffia, tied tautly cross-wise outer rim to outer rim, providing a basket weave foundation for a material to be placed upon it for security and five odd, half inch long 'leg like' squared wires wrapped around the main circular wire. Fourth, was the material in a bag, sealed shut, as if an ordinary bologna sandwich in a Spider Man lunch box. Well, to Brian, Spider Man was ordinary; but the content of dirt with tiny sprouts made a fairy tale of bean stalks sound feasible and infantile. Why climb to meet a villain, when an ally can grow in the backyard?

The last item, under the tool, wire rim, and bag of soil, might have been the most precious of all. Ten directions. One long piece of paper, much the size of a manila envelope, supplied ten simple instructions. Simple, uncomplicated applications---like the Ten Commandments.

The ad no longer existed. Brian scanned the pages of the comic book. Poof - gone. He understood the meaning---Be thankful for the pizza box, kid. You got one slice of the pie.

Brian refused to browse the instructions. Instead, savoring one by one. Each one on its own, unique chocolate.

Number One: Lay the wire hoop near a window, unobstructed. And place attached metal wire outward.

Books, pens, notebooks, instantly were removed from the three drawer wood desk at the south window of his bedroom, and shoved in the corner with dream items gone astray: roller blades and ice skates. Laying the wire flat, the five squared attached features gave the circle a star image. Refraining from cleaning with chemicals or detergents, Brian removed his grey soccer ball printed T-shirt, turned it inside out, and wiped any residue off the surface of his desk. He stood back, bent down, and eyed the desk for dust. Nothing, except the microscopic smear of his DNA. Perfect.

Number Two: Remove dirt from bag. Spread evenly inside the wire and spread gently with rake not disturbing the netting.

If Brian had spread the soil more gently, it would not have spread.

Number Three: Let faucet run exactly three
minutes at room temperature and at a slow flow.
Carefully fill enclosed cup half full.

Peeking out his room, Brian heard rattling of pots
and pans. His mother was in the kitchen. A three wall
barrier between them.

In the upper right dresser drawer rested a hodge-
podge collection of objects. The collage signifying
normality and sadness of disunion. Most items, unused.
A compass, pocket knife, lighter, hankie, plastic comb,
a rubber ball from a gum machine, a miniature yellow
flashlight, and one baseball card, of Bob Gibson, top
St. Louis pitcher in the 60's (To Brian, he didn't need
another, until cards of Mud Man printed) and finally a
stop watch.

Brian retrieved the stop watch, shoved it in his
front pocket and with the cup cradled in both his hands,
he maneuvered to the bathroom sink. He didn't have to
go far. Only twelve steps away in the small slab house.

Keeping the cup guarded in one hand, he spun
both knobs of the faucet. One then the other, until the
temperature blended into the air. He clicked the stop
watch and waited.

THREE MINUTES!

With surgeon's precision, he filled the cup.
Fearing he'd disrupt the water or rip the cup, he kept the
water running and returned to his room.

Number four: Dribble on dirt covering entire area.

Rake gently not disturbing netting.

The pounding of his heart entered his throat and caused a tightness fighting a tickle. Pure will denounced a cough, sniff, or swallow in close proximity to the dirt. Must not contaminate. Must not contaminate.

Number four was over. He stepped back five feet. Took a breath. Swallowed, and scratched his neck leaving three red marks chin to Adam's apple. He glanced at the directions, but only the next one. Number five would be murder. Why did the word pop? He hated that word. It alluded to evil. He preferred defeat.

Number Five: Wait twenty-four hours.

He'd defeat twenty-four hours. A call to supper resonated. If questions to the dirt arose, it was merely a project. Certainly, not a lie.

Shuffling to the bathroom, he shut the water off. A crooked smile formed as his lazy eye widened. He then consumed a hearty meal of beef stew and large slice of Mississippi mud pie. How fitting.

Living in dog years, twenty-four hours turned into a week. Teachers babbled, his mother whined, and yet the teasing on the playground twisted into a level of unconcern.

Resolved tranquility by looking ahead and ignoring the present. No issues, no fretting. Brian was onto direction number six.

He read number six twice.

Number Six: Gently raise the wire and engage the five attachments as a stand allowing air under the wire.

In the quiet of the room, his brain played band music. Mostly, trumpet and tuba.

Done.

Number Seven: Carefully repeat numbers three, four, and five.

His head pounded--Are you kidding? Torture. Mental torture. What was at stake? At the worst, residence in an institution muttering in Latin, though never learned. Eating springs on a bed, never realizing they're non-digestible, and dancing with a rat named Delilah, which unfortunately does exist. He'd watched a documentary on insane asylums. But really, how different is it for a gimp, cross-eyed, potty pants thrown into a classroom, an arena of sorts, of salivating gladiators.

At best, a test of patience. A test of competence. How bad did he want the reward? Mud Man expects no less. If he couldn't obey, why waste his time? The Pyramids, the Coliseum, the Taj Mahal, are not only structures of intelligence and endurance, but devotion. Devotion. Devotion.

He followed Number Seven, not reading number eight. Don't look ahead. Don't presume. He never pondered the use of the five attachments. Never guessed the why's and what fors. He'd just follow faithfully.

Only a few instructions remained.

Talk about bladder restraint, excitement pushed his organs to the max. He saw it. Immediately entering his bedroom after school, he saw it. After two harassing recesses and a drawn out lunch, where his apricot and grape jelly sandwich was taken, tossed about, and stomped on until the jelly overtook the bread, he saw it. Sprouts.

Tossing his book bag, he went to the window, dipped and inspected the wire. Roots were growing. Not from the top, but from underneath in the space. Growth. Roots reaching for ground, nutrients, life. His bladder expanded, he quickly went to the restroom, washed, wrung and sanitized his hands, and swiftly returned running his finger to number eight.

Number Eight: Carefully pick up wire and plant outside root down in healthy soil, partial sun.

For the first time since reading the directions, he curiously jumped ahead to the next instructions before finishing the prior.

Number Nine: Leave alone for twenty-four hours.

Twenty-four hours now seemed inadequate for what was to occur. Twenty-four hours. So close to success. So close to failure. So close to knowing. But he did know. And optimism grew with the sprouts.

Before he picked up the wire, he retreated five steps. Like a pre-game warm-up, confidence builder, cheer squad chat, he took a breath, swallowed, and scratched his neck leaving three red marks, chin to

Adam's apple. Some might call the routine a nervous affliction; Brian stuck with a winning game plan. Only his opinion mattered. As he stared at the roots, he reassessed. Mud Man and his. He reassessed again, returning to one opinion mattered. MUD MAN.

Luck (or Mud Man) was on Brian's side. He heard paper rumple, his mother go into the bathroom, and the door shut. Reading material, probably the newspaper. Meaning: A lengthy stay. Even with his slow pace, slower now that he was carrying precious material, he'd make it out the door before questions were asked.

The hours between directions gave time to search and analyze a proper, reverent location. In the woods behind Brian's house, not quite the atmosphere of the poster, sprawled two miles of wilderness and one cabin, housing Boy Scout memories. Though Mud Man deserved no less than the Tongass Forest, a sparrow's song kept in rhythm with 'From the Halls of Montezuma', the aroma of a musk rose pleasantly arrived like dew, and delectable morel mushrooms fed man and beast. In this squared, petite environment - snuggled between highways, subdivision, and factories - would be the epitome of sanctuary and protection. Small or spacious, enjoy. Mud Man went where needed. Indiscriminately, maintaining peace. No acre restrictions. No estate mandates.

Brian glided from his room. His gait light, the tension resting in his hands gripping the wire. Dragging a foot and seeking manual pressure; securing, but not disrupting fragile dirt particles and bristles of roots, especially from the underside, not an easy task. Factoring in the mental scrabbling of caution and fervency, he cracked the dial of challenged. He'd faced challenges his whole life. This one he accepted.

Ten yards out his back door, the terrain changed. Ruts, deeper ruts, then a complete drop of three feet. Now balance took center stage. He couldn't bear to remove one hand from the wire. The grip succeeding in lodging the wire against his chest and not jostling semi moist, yet loose soil. One wrong degree of thrust and it'd either plunge like a brick or spring up as if a flipped pancake. Nah, ah. Couldn't risk either.

So when meeting the severe drop, he eased into a sitting position on the edge and slid downward using his back and legs as worthy conductors, and relinquished scraped elbows and a light blue striped T-shirt with already a grape juice stain. Minor sacrifice, considering the option. Now back to the devices of ruts, deeper ruts, and fallen and low hanging branches. His destination was nearly a half mile out. With arm muscles twitching, a foot as a separate entity, and the anxiety that one clumsy maneuver and Mud Man was relegated to mangled marsh, a half mile is the devil's obstacle course of hell. Enter here. Food, gas, lodging, and peace of heart and soul a half mile away. The penalty of falling is never standing up. And neither does Mud Man.

Not wanting to feel rushed, Brian kept the stop watch at home. It had already served a vital purpose. But stuffed into the right front pocket of his jeans were the compass, lighter, pocket knife and flash light. The sky as blue as the artificial azure hair comb, his energy at a 'pitching nine inning shut-out' intensity, and the rubber ball wrapped in a hankie, tucked in his back pocket. The drawer of uselessness on its first field trip. A jaunt overcoming the stigma of inadequacy. A true 'never give up' rebel yell.

Ahead, the rusted gutters, chipped brown paint, and beacon of years gone by came into view. Once Brian saw the old cabin, yards turned to feet. Treachery teetering on victory. But he wasn't there yet. Ruts. Hidden-by-leaves ruts. Devil's last spikes to flatten the tires.

And then he arrived at the spot. He expelled air equivalent to one lap underwater at the city pool. Easy way to monitor--- slight dizziness, bulging eyes, a hint of panic, inflamed ears and cheeks, and exhilaration incomparable and insurmountable. Suddenly, that exhilaration diminished, as Brian gazed at the location of honor.

An old oak tree, sturdy, tall, proud, displaying nature's wisdom, longevity, and grandeur. How many storms had it defied? How many trapeze acts had it enjoyed? How many birds called it home? Multiple branches, all welcoming and lovingly conveying the warmth of a grandmother's hug. Yes, Brian pictured Mud Man rising, if for nothing else, to extend a 'thank you'.

Brian gave the sky a kiss disguised as a glance. The tree a hug disguised as a tap. And then planted the wire. Not disguising Mud Man's residency.

Three hours and fifty-six minutes into attempting a night's sleep, Brian fell asleep only to awaken by thunder twenty-two minutes later.

Snap. Light blinked at the darkness of his window, and then thumped and hit the roof in waves. Bold waves, crashing then subsiding, as the wind decided the course and Mother Nature pitched the fever. She was in a sickly moody tonight. Dribbles plinking the metal and glass, only to be replaced by plump rain with the force of pebbles. What did this mean for Mud Man's first night of propagation?

Insomnia joined the orchestra of weather and worry. Was it possible for Mud Man to be swept away? Drown if not rooted? Why, oh why, hadn't Brian researched botany? Biology? For heaven's sake, he'd researched cannons and the history of bottle caps, for meaningless school jargon, which would be forgotten in weeks and added no value to his life. But this, the most prized undertaking and event, able to change the course of environmental preservation and human suffrage, he neglected. Moron! He hadn't even listened to a weather forecast. He had one shot and he blew it. Put the items back in the drawer, shut it, and return to your useless life.

Or wait, maybe the deluge was a blessing. A burst of water to pack in a miracle.

The edge of the bed touched the window frame. Brian scooted to the end of his bed, curled his legs underneath him, peeled the Venetian blind, and gazed outside helpless. He had diligently followed instructions to Number Nine. No going back, starting over, or revising the directions. No second-guessing the benefits or demise of rainfall. Seven minutes and five seconds later he fell asleep sitting up, nose peeking out from the blind.

His mom drove him to school. The windshield wipers on, pendulum shift, fast speed. Mother's Nature's moodiness, stalled at angry. A charcoal grey suffocating cloud cover reinforced the sentiment.

Normally, when the rain ended, Brian donned the yellow slicker from the closet and placed his red/blue/white plastic boat in the puddle at the end of the drive way envisioning a wayward cruise on Lake Michigan. Now, he'd have to up the scale. Pacific Ocean. The boat wasn't equipped for sea water. What did it matter? Today, cruise ships and choppy waves ranked non-existent to the survival of Mud Man. Once out of school, rain or shine, monsoon or tornado, he'd be at the oak surveying the damage. Or deciphering otherwise.

Recess was indoors. Even Doug refrained from blatant belittling in front of teachers. Instead quick elbows were thrown. Bruises replaced jeering, but the verbal stuff hurt more. Left scars. Imprints on the brain do more damage than on the skin.

When Brian arrived home, the rain softened to a mist. Mother Nature's nap time. Such an influx gets tiring.

Before he could grab a jacket, Brian spotted Doug coming down the sidewalk. Cage in hand, and by the menial expression on his face, whistling. Content to trap and terrorize. The very notion sickened Brian. Knowing Doug would be in the vicinity of weakened Mud Man caused a fury Brian suspected existed, but hadn't scratched. A boil of an itch mounted.

Even forgoing the jacket, Doug had several steps on him. But he'd be in his line of vision. What Brian lacked in physicality, he'd make up for in familiarity and sheer contempt. Don't underestimate determination coated in myrmidon. Many wars have been won by such motivation.

Doug's ignorance and cockiness bounced off his yellow baseball cap as he paraded into the thicker brush. Brian had movement and a ball of light to follow. He was slightly losing ground, but Brian had him dead on. There'd be a confrontation before Doug violated land or animal. Or worse.

Jumping down off the ledge, Brian produced a

gallop, shaking his bum foot and closing the gap. Ruts be gone, he feared them no longer. When Doug got to the oak, Brian had the element of surprise to halt further encroachment.

Doug slowed five feet from Mud Man, wiped the thick gunk from his rubber boots on a rock, and pondered where to place the cage, unaware of Brian's approach. And he called himself a Boy Scout?

"You're not leaving that cage anymore." Hands on his hips, tone assertive, both eyes squinting directly at Doug.

"What are you doing here, cripple?"

"You're not leaving the cage."

"Yeah? Well, I'm thinking I am and you'd be smart not to stop me." Doug chuckled. "But then, you ain't so smart are you, freak? Go limp on out of here before you get hurt."

"You can't come in here and do damage anymore."

Doug ignored him, lowered the rim of his hat, and eyed a spot. Not a spot, the spot. "Oh, I think right here by this Oak tree would work." Doug took a step.

Brian took two. The swiftness, at first, paralyzed Doug. Mouth and feet.

"No." Brian said, firm and controlled.

Eye contact in the animal world would never have played this long. Fight or flight, most likely a lock of horn or jaw to neck and then death and dinner for one. Eat or be eaten. But an extreme amount of silence hung in honor of confusion on how to proceed.

Doug finally spoke. "Have you lost your stupid mind? I'll jam you in this cage!"

Doug took another step. Brian took two. A space of two feet, give or take a foot, separated them. Talking--- what they had for lunch could be smelled. Or fear. Oddly, Doug breathed fear. He didn't know why.

"Take the cage home. Smash it. And don't come into these woods again. I'm telling you."

A snout, snicker, sigh, emitted along with a shake of the head. How could this freak stand up to him? Why was he even afraid? "Ain't gonna happen, cripple." A voice said 'put the cage where you want it'. Another voice, a stranger yet viable, screamed 'heed the warning.' Was this the voice of reason? Or cowardice? Neither had been tested extensively.

Willing to jump the fence, Doug turned to set the cage down. Only inches from Mud Man.

"I said, no!" Brian grabbed the cage and spun Doug from the area. Even with the force and strength behind Brian's rage, Doug only budged a couple inches, refusing to drop the cage. He'd bring it down on Brian's head if pushed, but letting go of the cage wasn't going to happen. His fingers clung to the tiny metal as if soldered.

Doug raised the cage in an attempt to hit Brian. Brian ducked, jetted his hip and nudged him in defense. The impact caused more of a stir than the prior enraged spin. Doug stumbled backward, cage still high in the air, and both his feet landed inside the wire. An immediate look of despair crossed his face. Brian had seen the expression before on TV. The movie Jaws. A bite of a shark. A leg floating to the bottom. Severed at the waist. Wow, big, big trouble.

Doug began to sink. In seconds his ankles were covered and the knots in his knees absorbed the last swish of air. "Oh, no. I'm sinking. Get me out of here."

Keeping the cage high, he attempted to move his legs. It was futile. No, detrimental. Cement set up around his feet and thighs. He twirled his waist. The descent hastened. Hadn't Doug read that fighting quick sand only quickened your death?

Stunned, Brian watched, frozen.

"Cripple! Do something."

Even slipping into oblivion, hoping for assistance, Doug spewed hate. Niceness, not in his make-up.

The ground hit his shoulders. Cage still high above him. Maybe a bird would fly in and whisk him from the ground. Once the grit reached his mouth, no fluke of survival wondered abroad for help. In fact, the birds chirped loudly. In code. Brian didn't know the code, but he got the gist.

The last of the wire cage sank. Eerily, Doug didn't scream and Brian didn't move. A weird transference jolted over the area. 'A reap what you sow' mentality. Mud Man at work. Always taking on different forms. Communication. Yet, heavy rain had the potential to turn mail order mud to quick sand.

At home, Brian read number ten.

Number Ten: Water. Wait. Hope.

He'd followed the instruction best as he could, but then he noticed fine print down at the bottom. Moving the paper inches from his nose, he read.

NOT FOR USE BY CHILDREN.

Oh, well. He didn't always follow directions.

Kates Baloons

by Norma Jean Lipert

I always thought that it was best to tell the truth
at all times. Now I'm not so sure. Here I sit, in a sparse
and dreary jail cell, contemplating my future. Time is
running out. I need to make a decision and I need to
make it quickly. The rest of my life depends upon it. Do
I tell the truth and end up spending the rest of my days
among the lunatics in a mental institution or do I lie and
falsely admit to killing my wife and spend them in prison
surrounded by criminals? Which is the lesser of two
evils? Regardless of my choice, I don't see myself living as
a free man in the future. My story is so far-fetched that no
one will ever believe it. Heck, I wouldn't believe it either.
Not in a million years.

For the record, I did not kill my wife. I loved
her. She was my best friend. We were married for almost
36 years and had two beautiful children and three lovely
grandchildren. She was the best thing that ever happened
to me. Sure, we had a few problems early on in our
marriage; all couples do. Over time we managed to work
things out and now our marriage was envied by most of
our friends.

We both had good jobs and were nearing
retirement. Kate worked in the Human Resources
Department at our local community college and I,

Spencer Hoffman, was Vice Principal of Westwood Middle School. We both drove cars that were fairly new and we enjoyed dining out frequently. Our home was in a nice neighborhood and the mortgage was paid off a few years ago so we were financially secure. I had no complaints or regrets. We finally reached a point where life was really good and we were looking forward to traveling and experiencing new adventures after retirement.

It's amazing how things can change so quickly and without warning.

It seems like only yesterday that Kate and I sat at the breakfast table, discussing her upcoming birthday while having our morning coffee. You could tell by the look on her face and the sound of her voice that she was facing it with a great deal of apprehension. Usually, she embraced each birthday with anticipation, like a child, filled with excitement at the thought of the celebration. This one was different. Over coffee she was telling me she felt so old.

Actually, she was whining. Kate doesn't whine so I knew she felt strongly about this. This was a big birthday for her, her sixtieth, and she was dreading it with a trepidation I'd never seen in her before. For two weeks, she complained about it, as if she could somehow escape the inevitable. Even her coworkers knew how depressed she was over this one. "Fifty was bad enough," she moaned, "but sixty is just plain old."

"Nonsense," I replied, trying to comfort her, "you know you look at least ten years younger. Kate, you're not old. Besides, sixty is a new beginning. Soon we'll both be retired. The kids are grown, and now it's time for us to enjoy life and travel and do all the things we couldn't do while we were raising the kids and working every day. I promise you, Kate, life will be good. You'll see. It'll be a new beginning for both of us."

A new beginning...I can look back now and see clearly exactly when it all started. It was the beginning of the end; the end of us and our wonderful life together. It all started with Kate's birthday. That morning she took extra care dressing for work, carefully choosing her outfit, making sure she didn't look "old and frumpy," as she put it. "I really dread going in to work today. I'm really not in the mood to celebrate, and I know the girls in the office will have a cake for me. I'll probably start crying," she said. "Don't be silly," I replied, "just go and enjoy your day. I'll see you when you get home, and we'll go out to dinner. I'll even take you to your favorite restaurant. Now go."

I gave her a kiss and stood at the open door, watching heras she walked down the driveway and got into her car.Sitting behind the wheel, she glanced back at me with apained expression on her face. Wearing a forced smile, she backed the car out of the driveway, turned to me, and waved.

I blew her another kiss and waved back to her and watched her drive away. I knew her coworkers would cheer her up.

They were a wild group and never missed a birthday celebration. There would be cake and presents. Kate loved presents. I had no doubt that she would be fine once she got to the office.

It was as I predicted. The moment Kate pulled into the driveway and got out of the car, I could tell by the spring in her step that her mood had changed. She entered the house carrying bags filled with gifts, wearing a smile that stretched from ear to ear. "There are balloons in the car. Can you get them for me?" she asked.

When I saw the balloons I had to smile. They were two big heart-shaped helium balloons; one red and one pink. Each one sported a smiley face. The balloons were a reminder that today was also Valentine's Day. Kate was born on Valentine's Day. I thought back to past birthdays and how Kate always insisted on having two gifts. She did not want her birthday and Valentine's Day combined into one celebration. She had me put the balloons in her office which was located near the front door, off the living room area, and she went into the bedroom to change her clothes for her birthday dinner date.

I decided to make her a nice before-dinner cocktail and while I was mixing her drink, she reappeared wearing a beautiful blue dress that accented her eyes. She was still smiling.

Suddenly, I noticed she was not alone. "Who's your friend?" I asked, pointing behind her.

Directly behind her, the red balloon was slowly bobbing up and down as if it were nodding its head or laughing. The long ribbon streaming from the bottom almost appeared to be dancing to music. It was quite comical, but, at the same time it was eerie. It seemed almost human.

When Kate looked behind her, I could tell she didn't find anything comical in it at all. "How did that get in here?" she asked.

"It must have followed you." I didn't see what the big deal was about the balloon being there, but apparently I was missing something.

"That's impossible," she said, "You put them in my office."

"I did put them in your office. Maybe he was lonely," I joked, making light of the situation.

She ignored my little joke and studied the balloon carefully. "I haven't even been in the office since I got home. How could it just come out of the office by itself? It would have to duck down under two doorways, one in the office and the other in the living room. That's just not possible. This is just plain creepy."

I had to agree. It was rather creepy, and I could find no reasonable explanation of how the balloon ducked under two doorways and made its way into the kitchen. "Come on,

Kate. Let's go eat. I'm hungry. Finish your drink.
I'll put the balloon back in your office and then we can
go," I said, in a feeble attempt to change the subject.

Kate stood at the kitchen counter and stared at the
balloon as I took it back to her office. She looked up at the
doorway, obviously still trying to figure out how the
balloon could duck under it and make its way out of the
room.

"Don't worry," I assured her, "I tied it
to your chair. It won't be going anywhere."

Once the balloon was out of sight, I managed to get
her to finish her drink. Moments later the incident was
forgotten.

We had a great night out and celebrated with a
nice dinner and drinks afterward. On the way home we
stopped at a little club not far from our house where we
listened to live music and danced. It had been a long time
since we danced together. It was really nice.

The next morning things became even more
bizarre, if that were possible. We'd just finished breakfast,
and as we were having our second cup of coffee, we talked
about the fun we'd had the night before. We vowed to
have a special night out once a month and call it our "date
night."

We finished our coffee, and I started to load the
dishwasher. Kate went into her office to
get a few things she needed to bring to work that day. All
of a sudden I heard an ear-piercing scream. It was a

scream of sheer terror and it came from Kate. Startled, I almost dropped one of the dishes I was placing into the dishwasher.

I ran toward her office to see what caused her to scream. Kate came toward me, her eyes opened wide. She grabbed my hand and pulled me toward the living room. Before I could say one word, she said, "Come look at this. You're not going to believe this."

I must admit, it totally baffled me. The red balloon had once again escaped its home in the office. It was in front of the living room window, facing out, almost as if it was looking for something or someone. "What the...," I stammered, but before I could continue my sentence, the balloon turned at the sound of my voice and leered at me. The big smiley face that I once thought cute now appeared grotesque as it bounced up and down, sending chills up and down my spine.

"You said you tied it to my chair," Kate said, accusingly.

I had tied it to the chair. I could see no possible way that it could have gotten loose on its own.

"I did tie it to the chair. This is really strange. I don't know how it escaped," I replied.

"That's it. Get them out of here," Kate yelled. "Get rid of both of them. And why is it only the red balloon that keeps getting out and moving around? Why isn't it ever the pink one? It scares me. I know they're only balloons, but it's just too weird. I want them gone when I get home," she insisted.

I told her she was being silly. After all, it was just a balloon.

"I'll just break them and get rid of them." As soon as I said it, I realized my mistake.

"No!" Kate shouted, "you know how I feel about that." She had a look of pure horror on her face. I had forgotten that as a child Kate spent her summers with her grandmother. I remembered her telling me about her grandmother's superstitions and how she didn't fear the things most people feared - black cats, breaking a mirror, walking under ladders, things like that – but there were two things she felt strongly about. One was opening an umbrella indoors and the other was intentionally breaking a balloon. She believed they brought bad luck and unleashed trapped spirits. Before she died, she made Kate promise not to do either of those things. At the time I didn'tgive it much thought.

"Oh, Kate, I'm sorry.

I forgot. They're filled with helium so I'll just let them go outside."

She looked relieved and grabbed her purse. As she started out the door, the balloon turned toward Kate with a menacing stare. I was glad Kate didn't see it.

As soon as Kate left, I quickly put the red balloon in her office with the pink one until I could dispose of both of them.

I finished getting ready for work. This little fiasco

meant

I would be late today. Being a man of my word, I rushed into Kate's office to retrieve the balloons. I grabbed the pink balloon first and dragged it by its streamer to the front door. "Out you go," I commanded as I pushed it gently out the door. It shot up quickly into the air, reaching for the clouds. Within seconds it was no longer in sight.

"Now for the trouble-maker," I declared as I returned to Kate's office. Quickly, I grabbed the streamer and once again headed toward the front door with the evil culprit bobbing behind me. As I approached the front door, the balloon resisted, as if someone were pulling it in the opposite direction. The closer I got to the door the stronger the pull became.

I opened the door and the balloon suddenly pulled itself backwards with such force that the streamer sprang from my hand and found refuge in the corner of the living room. Surprised, I looked out the front door. Had a sudden gust of wind moved the balloon? All was still. Nothing stirred, not even a gentle wind.

I closed the door and went back to retrieve the runaway balloon. I glanced at the clock and remembered that I had a meeting scheduled with the other Vice Principals in less than half an hour. I couldn't be late. Not today. I decided to deal with the balloon when I got home, confident

I would arrive home before Kate.

No such luck. As fate would have it, Kate's car was in the driveway when I arrived home. "Oh, no," I said to myself, "I'm in big trouble now." I took a deep breath and braced myself for the sound of Kate's voice, knowing she would be very angry at me for not disposing of both balloons. Strangely, upon entering the house, I was greeted by silence.

"Kate, honey, I'm home," I announced loudly, thinking she might be in the bedroom changing her clothes.

No response.

"Kate?" I repeated.

Still there was no response.

Where was she? I glanced to my right, into Kate's office, and sighed. She sat in her high-backed chair in front of her computer, her back to me. I began to think she must really be mad at me and was not going to talk to me.

I stepped into her office, armed with my explanation, when suddenly my whole world collapsed. I could not believe the horror before my eyes. Kate was slumped in her chair. Coffee was spilled all over her keyboard and was running down the side of her desk. The cup was lying on its side. I stepped closer. Then I noticed her eyes. They were wide open, bulging with terror. She looked as if she were gasping for air or trying to scream. Blood trickled out of the corner of her mouth. I touched her arm and it was cold.

Kate was dead.

Then, I noticed the balloon. The thin red streamer, like a cord, was wrapped tightly around Kate's neck. The room spun around me as I staggered into the kitchen to call 911. I really can't recall the events that followed. It was like a dream. I was in shock. Vaguely, I remember opening the door for the emergency team. The silence was replaced by the sounds of people rushing back and forth from all areas of the house. Someone led me out of the room and sat me in a chair. Someone else had called the police.

The next thing I knew the police were asking me questions. I don't remember what I said to them. When I told them about the balloon, they glanced at each other with raised eyebrows. Nothing made any sense. They told me to come with them and gently ushered me out of the house. As I passed Kate's office, I couldn't resist glancing over. Someone was taking pictures. Then he cut the streamer from her neck, setting the killer balloon free.

As I was led to the police car, I noticed movement from the living room window. I looked up only to see the balloon at the front window once again. It was watching me. I called out to the police, yelling for them to look at it, but they ignored me.

"Look," I insisted, "it's laughing at me."

Again, they exchanged glances and shook their heads.

As the police car pulled away, I took one final look at the balloon in the window. It was still smirking as it bobbed up and down. It was still laughing at me. I swear I saw it wink at me, but who would believe me?

Now I have to decide the rest of my life in just a few short minutes. I hear the sounds of their footsteps growing louder as they approach my cell. I hear someone mentioning my name. Time is running out. They are coming to question me once again. What do I say?

Suddenly I hear a faint sound coming from the direction of my jail cell window. I look over at the bars with disgust. I should not be here. I am a well respected man in the community.

Scratch, scratch. There it is again. The sound was soft but distinct. Then I see something fly past my window. I got up from my bed and walked closer to get a better look.

I get a sick feeling in the pit of my stomach as the streamer passed by once again and I catch a glimpse of the red balloon.

No, it can't be.

As I strain my neck to the side to get a better look, the balloon suddenly dips down and hangs, suspended from the window, starring in at me.

I can hear only screaming. The scream of a madman. It wouldn't stop. It just kept on and on.

Musicians & Maniacs

by Karen DeCapp

*C*harisma trumps talent. Neither surprising, nor a secret, in the money obsessed field of entertainment. Talent may be improved upon and found readily, but star quality....ah... star quality is lightning in a cave. With a seductive smile in the lens fluttering a heart and drawing scores of teary eyed fans, mansion number two on the East coast is purchased. But stardom questioned fairness. To those living large, injustice was easily dismissed. To true artists, like Nick Sheppard, dismissal meant death.

A recording studio recognized an upcoming rock band had the current technologically advanced generation intrigued in a cult manner similar to the 1960's band 'The Doors'. Many sociological and physiological comparisons are tone driven. Today, youth entente and text messages punch songs into dynamite. Major youthquake. Communicate and violate. An altered state of mind, edgy lifestyles, and music with multiple, yet self-interrupted meaning, blasted into a mike spiraling the under thirty crowd into a tizzy. What irks the old, entices the young. Nick found the scene cliché.

Nick Sheppard wrote the music and lyrics for the soul quaking four man band 'Mental'. The title was derived from Nick's fetish with control. More precisely, telepathy. How much did the beat of the drums, pick of the guitars and ultimately the suggestion of the moody words effect the vulnerable thinker? That question and striving to possess and alter behavior elevated Nick from eerie to enigmatic. And knowing he was close to the capability made him dangerous. Unfazed and untiring, this was being done under the ignorance of the band members and the recording executives.

Lead singer, Samuel Dowell, comprehended Nick's composing talent. Nick constructed and was the foundation, but stage and lights belonged to Samuel. Without Samuel, promoting the group was like selling Playboy magazine without pictures. Some buyers read the articles as well as marvel at the bodies, but all leer at the nudity. And Samuel was the centerfold. He knew it, the promoters knew it, and Nick knew it. But acknowledgment wasn't acceptance according to Nick.

Women swooned over Samuel, platform boots to spiked hair. Such brass attention might have been a debilitating cut to the Achilles heel, or choleric ego of Nick, if not for one element. An element equipped with long auburn hair, eyes that mysteriously transformed from sable to azure to emerald like a buffed rolling marble, and a patient, kind demeanor rivaling the lead in a sappy romance novel. And this 'element' even had a Goddess name. Adella.

Nick was unsure what he'd fallen in love with

first--- name, face, or soul mechanics. The chicken or the egg, what does it matter? An existing, fully-embodied creature stood before him. He'd fallen and was a novice of rapture.

He was, however, uncertain if the commencement proceeded in unison. But they had entered the qualifying hand in hand—hadn't they? His signals read a seductive, yet unjaded smile cross her mouth when she saw him. A light tender laugh projected when he quipped anecdotes, and the tilting inward motion of her body read 'friends now, lovers later, and mates forever.'

Samuel's feast of disease infested, slutty groupies dished a banquet of bugs and blisters. Nick treasured the irony of popularity, allowing Samuel the menu of vermin, a dollop of penicillin, and an on call physician. Adella delivered a classic, devoted dish.

Two members of the band exited studio B3 after four hours of recording a three minute and forty-two second song. Fine tweaking was at a feverish pitch. 'Mental' instrumentally needed technology to sound premiere and so did Samuel's voice, though at concerts and in hotel rooms, fans didn't complain about the discrepancy. Flummoxed whores and druggies clamored for a piece of Hollywood, no matter the price. Samuel was riding the hurricane's wave. No moderation and no fear. The dream bubble of stardom floated along the sands of paradise. Not all members of 'Mental' enjoyed the carefree breeze. To Nick, nothing had the right to be carefree.

Samuel and Nick remained in the studio and hashed out plans to go over the newest song to the CD.

"How about ten o'clock?" Samuel was a night owl, as well as a sexual vulture. "Too late for ya, Nicky?"

"I'll be there."

Nick didn't make eye contact. Samuel's only calculable droning would be done on a mattress before Nick's arrival.

"This will give me time to work-out." Samuel said patting the six pack hiding under his hundred dollar T-shirt reading 'What you can't see, can hurt you'. "The ladies love looking at the rock gut on stage. Diligent training, no sugar, and limited carbs." Samuel mockingly tapped Nick's stomach. Nick pushed his hand away in objection. "You're lucky, Nicky. That guitar you play with mediocrity conceals the flab. See ya at ten." Samuel left.

Nick viewed Samuel flavorless without him, but wasn't naïve. Weighty record contracts hid farce calibrations. When millions are shelled out, millions show courtesy. Forced fake partnership. Does one bite of apple dipped in peanut butter and one bite dipped in chocolate alter the flavor of the apple? Trouble was, both considered themselves the apple, not the replaceable dip.

To Samuel, Nick was sour and rotting the sweetness. Approval of Nick's music or lyrics was meaningless. The only screeching more deafening than Samuel was Nick, and Nick didn't have the swagger to vitalize 40,000 ticket holders. As for Samuel composing a note or word, he couldn't identify a clef on sheet music or derive two words from the letters of 'misspelled'. But image is more than everything, it's the only thing. Fanfare to fan club.

Nick used the freedom of Samuel's condescension to review the session. Thirty minutes later he exited the studio. Two steps down the corridor, Adella turned the corner and appeared before Nick like an angel trailing a wish.

"Adella...." Nick said in a fantasy infused stupor, although it was not unusual seeing her in the recording studio. Her father was a top executive. Adella's majestic aura superceded breeding. Certain attributes derive naturally. Money and power are mere superficial projections. In her presence, Nick hit kundalini and a sixth charka, which is a profound yogi poise and non-touch transference. When she spoke he hit seven---total enlightenment.

"Nick, how nice to see you." Number seven received.

"You too."

"I bet 'Mental' is busy with their next CD, huh?"

"Oh, yes. Busy, busy."

"You're so talented Nick. Your songs reach many people, on multiple levels."

Nick's mind flashed—if only she knew.

"It's rare. I've been around music my whole life, and this band has magic. Long lasting magic." She paused to giggle girlishly and then tossed her tresses over her right shoulder. Nick watched, mesmerized. "In this business, that's a treasured commodity." She added.

Nick glanced at his watch. "Adella, I'm going to grab a bite to eat. Would you join me?"

"I'd love too."

"Great, you pick the place."

"Hmm...are you hungry enough for D'Stello's?"

D'Stello's was a romantic, candlelit, limited seating, waiter with a towel over his forearm, 'we embrace each other' cozy bistro. Nick quickly replied "Oh, yes." So he'd be late to meet with Samuel. The extra time would allow the raising and buckling of his pants.

"Okay, mind if I meet you there?" Adella asked.

"No. I'm on my way. See you there."

Twenty minutes later, Nick was pouring wine and an appetizer of shrimp and crab stuffed portabellas simmered at the table, along with Nick's libido.

Adella stroked the long stem glass in a provocative manner, before taking a sip.

"You know Nick, I have to say my favorite song of the band's is 'Can't do it without you.' My spirit dances." She placed her hand over Nick's and the spiritual dancing continued. "Did it take you long to write?"

"Huh..." Nick was swaying in and out of coherence

because of the electricity surging. With a blink, shoulder twitch, and bottom lip bite, he reentered the conversation. "I think just a night or two. When I focus, I can create quickly."

After the consumption of two zesty ziti's, the last drop from the bottle of wine, and the flirting of reaming pupils, Adella broke the carnal vibe and explained she had to leave because of a prior commitment.

"How about dinner tomorrow night, Adella?"

"Tomorrow? Oh, I can't, but I can the following night. Will that work for you?"

"Yeah, I'll pick you up at 8:00."

"Remember the address?"

"Oh, yes." Nick had taken Adella home from the studio on one occasion. But return trips had been several. A history of numbers, lights, and stairwells formed explicitly. Two blocks north, eight blocks east, corner grey structure between another apartment and a dry cleaners with a red neon light flashing '24 hour service'. An intercom with a gold button and a silver speaker was at the entrance, a bordered rust/brown rug needing to be vacuumed neither in a country nor Victorian decor was in the foyer, and the elevator to the third floor was twelve steps to the right. Apartment 314 was three quarters of the way down the hall with numbers in gloss black bookman old style font. If he took the stairwell, he climbed seventy-eight steps, and took thirty-four full strides until the peephole lined up midway at his nose.

The only thing more vivid than the journey to her home was how her hand felt on his. He'd fallen in love. Not obsession---Love.

For now, he had to refocus. A pretentious, phony encounter was to take place with the no talent, sexually consumed Samuel. Yes fame and money had fallen into the lap of 'Mental', but how long before the tarot cards flipped 'revenge'? Nick was the avenger, and Samuel was the victim.

Excessive energy and vigilance was given to Samuel's physique. Samuel viewed his weakness for women as admirable, but weakness in his diet or an underachieved push up tally shattered the ego. A buff body meant supreme stamina buffing chicks. Samuel held pride in his rigid food consumption.

Nick planned to clog the lean jugular. Game on. Assault arrogance. This prompted Nick's current insidious music manipulation. Monitoring heart rate and lung expansion with specific pitches and rhythms orchestrated cerebral action. How often do you hear rap at yoga sessions? Classical music at dance clubs? No mind and body fusion occurs. Task at hand: Must precipitate a subdued connection.

He learned to keep fluid communication intact, along with decibel pitches, allowing words to persuade. Words to control. And the manner and loudness in which they're delivered are cerebral markers. The oh-so genre of brain washing possesses the spirit. One only has to watch tribal ceremonies to comprehend how pounding and chanting delegate willpower. Lost in the thumping, nuance falls prey.

Where Samuel had the presumed upon self-restraint to reject a cookie, his mind failed in deflecting recourse. Or to go further, Samuel didn't have the intellect or any sense to expect a subconscious combatant. Conclusion: a perfect target. His savvy relied on muscle and material.

Nick believed in bending spoons with a stare, visiting dead relatives via Ouija, and presenting a CD invoking finely tuned pitches and lyrics inspiring a simpleton rock singer and fitness guru to eat donuts and pie. And the evidence would be in Samuel's hand tonight.

*   *   *   *   *

get me doughnuts----get me sweet potatoe pie
gotta have 'em-----gotta eat 'em
gotta have a complete white sugar high

Gluttony, coercion, and perversion were grooved into a disc, which Nick smugly gripped in his left hand, as he knocked on the door of Samuel's penthouse. Precise tone, fever, and tribal voodoo rested in one song. A test of power was underway. Power to dominate, seize, and take down the enemy.

Samuel opened the door with a towel wrapped

around his waist. "Crap, is it time already?"

Nick stepped inside "Oh, yeah—it's time."

Appearing from the hallway leading to Samuel's bedroom was a stringy-haired blonde waif in matching red lace panties and a bra. Her breasts pushed past the realm of being real and the ability of the underwire.

"Samuel?" She called in a sultry manner.

"Get dressed and get out. I have to work now."

Her eyes widened. "You working on a new song?"

"I said get dressed and get out."

She sighed and disappeared down the corridor.

"Tell you what, Samuel. I burned off the new song. Take a listen and let me know your thoughts tomorrow." Nick set the disc on the chrome and glass coffee table. "We have a 9:00 am session in the studio." Not waiting for an answer, Nick turned to leave.

"Hey Nick.."

Nick looked back. Deep in thought, Samuel asked "Do you believe in connections? A conflict, like water and oil, yet it blends?"

Squinting, Nick pondered his question. Was it a male bonding attempt? Was he finally acknowledging Nick's importance? "Yeah, sure---listen to the song. See ya tomorrow."

One good deed might result. If Samuel listened to the song with the ninety pound freak, she'd eat.

*   *   *   *   *

The always punctual Nick arrived at the studio ten minutes late. Samuel, normally loving a grand late entrance, awaited Nick.

Once Nick entered the booth of seismic knobs and dials, a smile not of 'a cat that ate the canary', but 'a warrior that conquered an empire' emitted with a mere tilt of the lips and one eyebrow raise.

At least a half dozen plates and pie tins lined the shelf of the glass control center. The two other band members stood stunned as Samuel sat and shoveled a fork into his mouth with a heaping spoon of sweet potato pie.

Seeing Nick enter, one replied "Look at this Nick. 'Love my body Sammy' is eating junk like it was his last day on earth. Unbelievable."

"Not really." Nick mumbled.

"Huh?"

"Nothing." A bizarre look flashed from Samuel at Nick from over the spoon. Nick continued. "So you had a sweet tooth today, did you?"

"Can't get enough." Samuel's voice was hoarse and hypnotic causing a deeper grin and a higher brow on Nick.

"Sorry I'm late guys. I'm going to make a quick trip to the restroom and we'll get this show on the road." Nick left. He walked to the restroom and studied the mirror and the genius staring back. "You are in control, buddy."

After taking care of business and the pep talk, Nick left the restroom and six feet away Samuel was embracing a woman. In his view was Samuel's back side and thin, yet toned arms of a female wrapped around him with one hand on his upper back and one squeezing the denim pocket of his jeans. Nick sighed. It had taken seconds for animal mating season and a floozy with red nail polish to disrupt and deride the sanctity of the studio.

"C'mon give me a break." A flippant demeanor flowed.

The two broke up the make-out session. Samuel turned around and the woman stepped to his side. They stood arm in arm.

A thunderous bolt, like a lever pull of an electric chair, seared through Nick's body. No part of his being went unaffected. With the surge of voltage, his existence departed the core and mitigated to dust. In powder form the pain disarmed. Or so he thought.

Standing before him, tightly molding to Samuel was Adella. Embarrassed only for necking in the corridor like a teenager, Adella lowered her eyes and gently brushed her lips. "I guess that was a tad inappropriate. I'm sorry."

Oblivious to the heart wrenching collapse of Nick's soul, Samuel asked. "You've met Adella, haven't you, Nick?"

"Good to see you again, Nick." Adella said with

the identical tone, that only hours ago meant 'I want to be with you the rest of my life.'

Nick didn't speak, as he envisioned the empty shell of his existence turning to sand and being blown away by a typhoon.

Adella spoke to Samuel. "See you tonight at 8:00?"

"You know it, sweetie. Love ya."

"Love ya too." They kissed and Adella placed her hand on Nick's shoulder as she walked passed. "It was good to see ya again, Nick."

A reflexive shrug of disgust ensued. Nick calculated his next mission. It'd take work, but if he believed it was doable----and he BELIEVED----it would occur.

Once Medusa was out of sight, Nick spoke to Samuel. "Why don't you go ahead and record with the band. I'll come in later and finish up."

"What, you nuts? We all have to play, man."

"No we don't. I have a song I have to finish. I'm the sole music and lyric writer, remember? It's a killer. The only place I can do this is in the confines of my home." Every word was true, and the meaning: cryptic. "I'll drop off the last addition to our new CD at 7:00. And I'll tie up the loose ends here. I'll take care of it."

Not waiting for an answer or debate, Nick raced out.

*   *   *   *   *

As Nick plotted, he recalled the manifestation of his ability. Aged nine, breathless and sweating from only the temple, he placed a feather found in his backyard by a trash can and under a large branch, into an unused mason jar and screwed on the lid tightly.

Peering at the spotty separation in the feather, he concentrated at the same tick of the clock every day. Five o'clock--before supper, before school work, and after outside play time. At first the sessions lasted five minutes, within weeks: an hour. And in a month, the feather moved. Not an eye-tricking float, but a jump. As if wanting out of the bottle and Nick's deadening stare. Or possibly, a wave hello.

Soon an obsession to further the incitement began. With his love of music, tempo, and control he broadened the command mechanism and tested the will of a victim.

'Caramel' their evil tempered tabby cat hated many things, but nothing more than water. Hearing the faucet turn and the stream emit, elevated the cat to panic mode with seclusion under a heavy piece of furniture. Music was the first to soothe the jitters. Next, calibrated rhythm and entranced lyrics guided Caramel out of the cave to protection of the couch or bed. But Caramel submerging into the tub, on its own, without the brutal fling of an agitated youngster took patience and perseverance. Nick was willing to donate and dedicate himself to the task. He had the calling. He moved the feather. He was a musical prodigy. All wove a sordid provocation to cause submission and without the culprit privy to the weakness. Most little boys dream of being able to fly, he dreamed of making others think they were able to fly. The magnificence of malice.

On a cold, snowy morning shortly after the celebration of a new year, Caramel, after hearing Nick's deliberate composition to influence her movements, strolled into the bathroom, sprang three feet high and jumped into five inches of bath water. Minus fear and minus hesitation, Caramel was the first bodied creature to succumb to Nick. Feather to fur. How difficult could humans really be? Most have to summon intellect to order fast food.

Never to nix curiosity, Nick pondered the owner of the feather. Researching birds, he became aware Blue Jays visited and nested in the yard. Blue Jays were notoriously arrogant and over-confident. They were the bullies pushing the smaller birds off the feeder. He'd wondered, was this the feather he'd elevated and controlled? Symbolism is subjective at best, and psychotic at worst.

Or had the feather belonged to a buzzard? These predators symbolized death and decay. Had the hopping and vision inside the jar held a reverse transition? The theory was preposterous. Dwelling on the when and why, depleted concentration. Nick couldn't have that.

Years later, Nick's capabilities were serving him as

he wished. And his wish was to seek revenge and inflict a lifetime of horror onto an enemy. Killing two birds with one stone, so to speak. Nick snickered at the analogy as he composed his lyrics:

Hold the knife, plunge the blade
Gonna spray this room in red. Can't fight the shade.
Won't stop till you topple and expel your last sigh
Don't seek forgiveness. You played me, therefore you must die

Tone, thumps, and suggestion were in order. Translating like anatomical teamwork of diaphragm and ribs contracting and creating a negative pressure or vacuum to force air through and form a breath. Tender internal gears shift and produce a double pump flush which in return forms one heart beat—just one. Even the alveoli of the lung drives the fist sized heart to function.

Nick didn't believe it was possible to over analyze. Major compliance, fragile balance, and conductor's skill are underway as we go about the day. Deliberate cognition is needed to pour a cup of coffee, but the brain directs our organs robotically. The system works, and works in unison. All vital. All simultaneous, and life and death depends on systematic cooperation. Add cerebral influence, which profoundly massages the soul subconsciously, and BINGO---Samuel will repeatedly stab Adella. Result: Death and vengeance, and to Nick a fitting finale. As simple and complicated as the body itself.

Though Nick despised Samuel, the animosity was unpreventable and unchangeable. But Adella was a betrayer plunging a sword into his back. They were supposed to marry. Love unconditionally. She'd misled, mocked, and ridiculed him. Her two faced transformation from devotion to whore was insufferable and punishable by death. The blade would be the source of her demise and the inflictor, her arrogant lover.

Samuel would be convicted and serve life in prison. Samuel—the pretty boy with the chiseled body surrounded only by men to worship his fame. Death wouldn't be his biggest nightmare.

Nick knocked on the door to Samuel's penthouse. Shirtless in tight black jeans, Samuel opened the door. Nick quickly placed the disc in his hand. "Here ya go. Play it when Adella's here. Get her opinion."

"I always do, Nicky."

"I'll see you later." Excitement accelerated saliva. Nick swallowed and wiped his mouth. He'd return about 9:00, witness the carnage, and call the police.

*   *   *   *   *

The door was ajar and only a filtered illumination sneaked over the threshold when Nick returned. Malignant signs the environment held a secret hung in the grayness as Nick entered.

In a light shuffle, he took two steps inside. A black mass cowered on the couch. Fast blinks and a pinch to the nose, Nick adjusted to the shadowy deception of the living room. Candles blazed and moonlight crawled from the thin gaps of the vertical blinds diffusing outlines and chaffing definitions.

Nick stopped and focused on the figure. It was Samuel. He was not cowering but hunched over, elbows on knee and clasping his head as if battling ear-drum-exploding shrieks.

Before speaking, Nick listened for music. Nothing. He listened for the movement of Adella. Nothing.

"Samuel?"

No response.

"Samuel? Everything alright?"

No response.

Nick, mindful of Samuel, glided past him as if he was a hissing snake coiled and ready to strike. But Nick sensed the serpent's deed was done.

As he approached the corridor leading to the bedroom, the clouded fun house lighting continued. Nick walked in a confident, but soft heel-to-toe rolling manner, down the distorted tunnel to the crime scene. There was no rush. No remorse. What had to be done was done. And as the bedroom loomed only inches away, his talent and power surged with raw primal adrenaline.

Halting at the doorway, he examined the room

and Adella. Candles flanked the furniture around the bed. And the bed served as Adella's final skin to material sensation before succumbing to a violent end. Face down, semi-nude, her gleaming auburn hair fanned out shrinking the width of her shoulders before cascading over the edge of the mattress. Her long legs consumed the lower section of the bed, seemingly out of proportion to her physique. Or were the flicks of light and Nick's internal rejoicing altering perception?

A kitchen knife was placed on the dresser.

As Nick's eyes scanned Adella's tomb and his emotions celebrated, omission scratched the vent of delusion. Something was amiss.

With a low scuffing sound behind him, Nick abruptly turned to encounter the wild stare of Samuel. Suddenly, the king of the jungle became the rabbit stalked by the wolf.

"Samuel? Did you hurt Adella?" Where was the splattering of red? The saturation of blood? Although the room was dim, the knife was clean. Completely clean! The silver of the blade reflected the flame of the candle.

Then from the bedroom, a familiar song played....

I am your partner. Joined by mystique
Whatever the hold. I cannot defeat.
Tied to you by love I will ensue
Follow you to hell.
Whatever you want 'I can't do it without you'

Nick had written that song months ago, and Adella expressed to him it was her favorite. His mind sorted through the timeline---When exactly did 'Mental' coercion begin? Had the lyrics of 'Can't do it without you', though unintended to control, infuse an unbreakable commitment between Samuel and Adella? Hearing it together now, and years ago for the first time, must have fused a bond. And ultimately, the pledge of partnership. In his egotistical absorption, he'd altered fate.

While Nick pondered the flaw of his power, Samuel raised a knife and plunged it into his chest. Nick's knees buckled and he collapsed. Weak and trying to hold the gush of fluid from his wound, he rose and took an unstable step only to find Adella in his way.

"Adella...."

She had retrieved the knife from the dresser and brought it to his neck. The impact sprayed red onto the walls, clothing, and a puddle of deep crimson grew on the floor like a shallow stream in a monsoon.

In seconds, Samuel and Adella swung their arms in madness. No emotion. No compassion and certainly, no signs of lethargy. Their attack was savage, like hungry wolves feeding on a carcass until Nick lie quiet. Thick reams of blood crept down the wall, swayed over the baseboard, and oddly writhed to their mangled owner.

Unyielding sentiment permeated from the song

riddling (buzzard-like) devotion and decay.

Samuel then said in a mesmerizing pitch, as if ready to break into song "You see, there's an unexplainable connection between me and Adella."

Nick had joined the two together. How mental.

.

Serenity Lane
by Jennifer Iacovoni

2004

Stacy

Stacy was so excited about her new home. She still could not believe the deal she got on it. She was approved for a HUD loan when she came across the tri-level, brick home on a two-acre lot surrounded by woods on the peaceful street named Serenity Lane. The house had been in foreclosure, and with the down payment provided as a gift from her parents for her up coming wedding, she was able to close the deal and move right in.

The house had been professionally decorated by one of the previous owners. But it just wasn't her style, so Stacy was thumbing through design magazines for inspiration. Stacy was lost in the world of before and after pictures when she heard a knock at the door.

Peeking out the peep hole in the door, she saw a woman with dark hair who looked to be about her age maybe a little older, holding a plate of cookies. 'How sweet,' she thought. 'A neighbor coming to welcome me to the neighborhood.'

"Hi ya'll! My name's Jeanette, I live in the house just up the road from you," she said. "I just wanted to stop by and welcome you to the neighborhood. May I come in?" she continued. Stepping back from the door, Stacy gave way to the visitor.

"My, this place hasn't changed a bit since they rebuilt it," the neighbor drawled.

"Rebuilt it?" Stacy asked.

"Oh, my sweet child," the neighbor said. "Don't tell me you don't know the history of this house. You best take a seat, this will take a while."

1998
Tim & Jeanette

They turned down the street and saw the house of their dreams. A tri-level built into a hill with a walk-out basement. Sitting back on a wooded lot, it was truly the picture of serenity that the street's name promised. They slowed and wrote down the phone number of the realtor. Talking excitedly, they continued to the end of the street. The sight there took their breaths away and turned their excitement into fear.

The house on the end of the street had obviously been lost to fire. The frame, or what was left of it, was charred; the second floor had collapsed into the first. The garage was a pile of rubble around the remains of a car. There must have been an accelerant used because the house was so completely destroyed.

"Did you see that?" Jeanette asked.

"What?" Tim asked in return.

"It looks like a sign," she replied. "Interesting. Let's check it out." Putting the car in park the couple climbed out of the car and approached the house. There was a sign hanging from the post near what must have been the front door frame. It read:

Please be respectful in this place. My husband lost his life in this fire. The tragedy that our family has suffered is more than which can be expressed in words. Only God can save us now.

With a chill running down her spine, Jeanette turned to Tim and said, "I don't like this honey, not one bit."

"Don't be silly," he responded "This ain't the house we're buying. Besides, you don't believe in ghosts and such, do you?" Jeanette didn't believe in ghosts, well not on that day anyway.

1998
Paul

When Paul's sister told him she was buying a house, he was excited. Her and her new husband had been looking for months. He couldn't wait to visit and found it odd that his sister didn't seem as excited to have him visit. He sensed that something was wrong. "What wrong with the house?" he pressed.

"Nothing," she replied. 'You'll see when you get

here,' she thought.

Later that week when Paul arrived, he knew at once what was bothering his sister. He was drawn to the house next door. He drove his car slowly past the house. As he did a chill ran up his spine and he felt a sudden sense of dread. Turning his car around, he headed back up the street. Then he heard and felt a sudden pop as the front right tire blew. Startled, he continued to creep slowly up the street when suddenly another pop rang out. This time it was the left rear tire. No longer concerned with the car, Paul abandoned it and ran for his sister's house.

There was something wrong with that house and Paul knew it. "Jeanette, what were you thinking buying this house next to that one?" he asked.

Jeanette sighed, "We got a great deal on this one. Besides, someone will rebuild it. I'm certain."

'But will it be soon enough?' Paul wondered.

1999
Tim & Jeanette

The house next door had finally been purchased and the rebuild had begun. Tim and Jeanette watched happily as they started to remove the rubble. "I told you that they would fix up that house, didn't I?" Tim said. He was right after all and it didn't take as long as Jeanette had worried.

"I'll sleep well tonight knowing that eyesore will soon be gone," she said with a smile.

Later that night when the couple was settling down to bed, Tim froze. "Did you hear that?" Tim asked.

"Hear what?" Jeanette asked.

"Oh, nothing," he said. But Tim was certain he heard something in the bathroom. Deciding to ignore it, they settled down to sleep.

"Ahhhhhhhhh!" Jeanette screamed out from a deep sleep. Startled, Tim jumped from bed and raised his arm, fists clenched and ready to fight off whatever it was that caused his wife's blood curdling scream. "Did you see him?" Jeannette asked in a panicked voice. "Did you see that man that was leaning over the bed?"

"No, there wasn't anyone in the room!" Tim replied.

"But there was! And he leaned over the bed and was staring down at me," Jeannette insisted with a quiver in her voice. Knowing they wouldn't go back to sleep, the couple went downstairs and brewed some tea.

Jeannette was certain that someone was in the room. 'Has the construction next door awaked the spirit of the original owner?' Jeanette wondered.

2000
Tracy & Phil

After her divorce, Tracy moved into the cutest house she had ever seen. A tri-level on a glorious two-acre lot; on a street named Serenity. What could be more perfect then that? She had read in the papers that the original home had burned in a fire. But this house wasn't a rebuild of that house; not really. That house was completely leveled and only the concrete driveway remained. Any misfortune or bad luck was surely removed with the rubble. Well Tracy never believed in spirits, or bad karma for that matter. She attended church on a regular basis and knew that souls left this earth upon death and went to either heaven or, God forbid, hell. She would hold this belief until she met and married Phil.

Phil moved in just after the wedding, and that's when the mood started to shift. A successful mortician for over 20 years, Phil had worked for the same company for most of career. But he was taken by surprise when he arrived at work one day and was told that his services we no longer needed, and he was to leave the premises. In shock, Phil returned home only to learn that Tracy was fired from her job as well. Neither of them was provided with a clear explanation as to why this had happened. In shock, they reviewed their finances and decided that they could manage about 6 months on savings. After that, they would most likely have to sell the house. Tracy cried herself to sleep that night. She loved the house and had spent a lot of time with a decorator getting it just the way she wanted it. While deep in sleep, Tracy was awaked by eerie sounds. What she thought was crying turned into wicked laughter. It seemed to be coming from all corners of the house.

The next day they put the house on the market.

2001
Linda & Tony

Linda and Tony had a good life in Chicago, but they were not against change by any means. So when Tony's company offered him a promotion to open their new location, he was up for the move. Arriving in a new city and state, Linda and Tony were eager to start house hunting. Linda had, in fact, started the search on-line. There was one house that had caught her eye. It was on the multi-list and had been for almost a year. It was beautiful and she really couldn't see anything wrong with it. After contacting the listing agent, they made an appointment to see the house. Driving down the street they were happy to see a few couples close to their age. The couple next door even waved as they drove by. "My! Everyone seems friendly around here." Linda commented.

"Yes," the agent replied. "This sure is a great little neighborhood." As they turned into the driveway, Linda and Tony instantly knew that this was the house for them. After moving in, Linda started to meet the neighbors. All were very nice at first, but they also seemed reluctant to talk about the previous owners. Linda would hear such comments as, "Nice people, bless their hearts. Just a shame what happened to them." And other comments such as, "You just never really know people." Determined not to let these comments bring her down, Linda set about making this new house her home.

One day after cleaning and organizing her kitchen, Linda decided to go for a walk in the woods alongside her house. Starting on a walk down the trail, Linda listened to the wind in the trees and the birds singing. She heard something move through the leaves nearby. Turning she saw a beautiful cat with shiny gray fur and the most beautiful blue eyes. Knowing a little about cats, she recognized it as a Russian Blue. A purebred cat like this would belong to someone nearby, and surely shouldn't be wandering the woods. Bending, she reached for the cat and tried to pick it up. But the cat scurried just out of reach, then stopped and looked back as if waiting for her to follow. Sensing no wrong, Linda followed. The cat led her just down the path to the edge of a creek. There, the cat started to scratch at something. Bending over to get a closer look, it appeared that there was sign buried in the dirt. Linda brushed away the dirt and read the sign.

Please be respectful in this place. My husband lost his life in this fire. The tragedy that our family has suffered is more than which can be expressed in words. Only God can save us now.

Feeling a little unnerved, Linda returned to the house to find her husband's car in the driveway. He was home early. That was odd.

Tony had been having pain in his throat when he ate. He had bad bouts of acid reflux before; but this was something new. Thinking that maybe he needed a new antacid medication to combat this new symptom, he had gone to the doctor earlier that day. But he was in no way prepared for what he was told. "I have cancer," he said to Linda. "Esophageal cancer," he explained. Linda sank into the couch, her eerie story of the sign suddenly forgotten.

2002
Jeanette

The house next door sat empty again. Tony's bout with cancer involved radical surgery and huge medical bills. Linda was so upset that they had to leave; but the house was going into foreclosure and their only hope was to move back home and stay with family. Though the surgery improved Tony's odds of survival, he wasn't completely out of the woods yet. Linda would have to find work in order for them to rebuild their lives. Before they left, Linda had stopped to say good bye. Jeanette, feeling over run with guilt for not mentioning it before, told Linda the story of the original house and the sign. Linda had turn sheet white as Jeanette shared the story. "What is it?" Jeanette asked.

Linda responded in a shaky voice, "The day we found out about Tony's cancer, I had been walking in the woods and a beautiful Russian Blue cat lead me to a sign covered in dirt."

"A sign?" Jeanette asked.

"Yes," Linda replied. "The same sign you just described."

Jeanette gasped and covered her mouth in shock. "My God" she cried out. "They had a Russian Blue cat that also died in the fire."

2004
Stacy

Stacy sat quietly and listened to the neighbor's story of tragedy that had befallen those who owned the house before her. She wasn't really sure how to react. She had her own beliefs and she was sure that nothing bad would happen to her or her loved ones. She was the third new owner after all. Don't they say the third time's a charm? Or is it three strikes and you're out? Maybe she should bless the house...or maybe not.

Author's note

Before starting to write this story I thought I would take a virtual walk past this house on Google Earth. Not sure what I'd find, I was pleasantly surprised to see that the house was still standing and was relatively unchanged. With one exception: attached to the front of the house, next to the front door and over what was the master bedroom of the original house, was an enormous wooden cross.

Author Bios:

Matthew C. Dampier is a short story author and songwriter who resides in Kansas City, Missouri. When he isn't entertaining his wife and young child, he occupies himself with the absurd and macabre.

Holly Day's published books include Music Theory for Dummies (translated into Dutch, French, Spanish, Portuguese, Russian, and German), Music Composition for Dummies, and Guitar-All-in-One for Dummies. She is a housewife and mother of two who teaches needlepoint classes for the Minneapolis school district and writing classes at The Loft Literary Center.

Karen DeCapp lives with her husband, Mike, and a 'tummy-rub' demanding mutt, Katie, in Coal Valley, IL, where morning runs produce high endorphins and dark stories. Having penned mystery and paranormal manuscripts, this is her first foray into short stories.

Jennifer Iacovoni Writer and mother of two Jennifer enjoys writing creepy tales that keep you up at night.

Norma Jean Lipert was born in Newark, New Jersey, but grew up all over the United States. She and her husband currently live in Texas. In addition to being a writer, she is also a professional clown, artist, and actress. She enjoys traveling and has visited many places both in and out of the United States. She has published three books and is currently working on several short stories and film scripts.